Other Books by Priscilla Cummings

A Face First

Saving Grace

Red Kayak

What Mr. Mattero Did

Chadwick the Crab

Chadwick and the Garplegrungen

Chadwick's Wedding

Chadwick Forever

Oswald and the Timberdoodles

Sid and Sal's Famous Channel Marker Diner

Toulouse: The Story of a Canada Goose

Chesapeake A,B,C

Chesapeake 1,2,3

Chesapeake Rainbow

Meet Chadwick

Santa Claws, The Christmas Crab

Beetle Boddiker

Autumn Journey

PRISCILLA CUMMINGS

For Lauren and Grace —

With best wishes,

Priscilla Cummings

2008

Published by Cornell Maritime Press/Tidewater Publishers.
Visit us at www.cmptp.com.

Library of Congress Cataloging-in-Publication Data

Cummings, Priscilla, 1951-

Autumn journey / Priscilla Cummings.

p. cm.

Summary: When his family comes to live on his grandfather's farm in Pennsylvania while his father is out of work, eleven-year-old Will must deal with his father's distant behavior, his grandfather's heart attack, and caring for a goose he has shot.

ISBN 978-0-87033-606-5 (pbk.)

[1. Grandfathers—Fiction. 2. Canada goose--Fiction. 3. Geese—Fiction. 4. Fathers and sons—Fiction. 5. Unemployment--Fiction.] I. Title.

PZ7.C9149Au 2008

[Fic]--dc22

2008032545

Manufactured in the United States.

For John

I wish to thank Larry J. Hindman, Waterfowl Program Manager of Maryland's Department of Natural Resources; my friend, Kathy Higdon, for helping me to see the "big picture;" and, especially, Ann Tobias.

*The geese are aloft,
piping their haunting
obbligato to the grander,
slower cadence of winter's
coming. It is music that
sets dogs to frenzied
yelping along the great
migration routes from
Labrador to North Carolina,
and makes people on
the streets of large cities
pause, cock an ear, and
look skyward, stirred by a
longing so old and deep
we cannot articulate it
much better than the
dogs....*

—Tom Horton,
author of
Bay Country

Contents

Escape

He never told anyone about it. And he'd be the first to admit it was kind of strange. But often, Will Newcomb liked to imagine he was a bird.

It all started a couple of years ago, in the third grade. There was a lot of waiting around in Will's noisy East Baltimore school. Waiting for things to quiet down, waiting for a teacher to finish yelling at some kid, *waiting* for the bell to ring. And so Will spent a good deal of time imagining himself as a bird, flying off to a quiet place that had acres of green grass and hillsides thick with trees. A place that, in Will's mind, always looked exactly like his grandfather's farm in Pennsylvania.

Summers, when he stayed a whole month at the farm, he built secret forts in the woods and raced his bicycle full tilt down the lane stirring up a huge cloud of dust. Once, he discovered a possum stuck in an empty silo and helped it escape by lowering a long tree branch inside, making a kind of ladder to the window. The possum hung on upside down and inched his way right out.

Like the possum, sometimes life was upside down, Will thought numbly as he plucked a piece of straw from the hay bale he was sitting on. Here he was, actually living at the farm and it was more like a nightmare than some wonderful dream come true.

"Will! It's time to go!" someone called from out in the yard.

Will cast an angry glance toward the front of the barn. He worried that, unlike his possum, this time there would be no escape, not even through his imagination.

"Will! Where are you?"

Throwing down the straw, he moved quickly, quietly, to the back of the barn, where he stood in a little room beneath the hayloft. Years ago, his grandfather stored the harnesses for his two workhorses here and the room still smelled faintly of leather and sweat. Will liked the smell, but he liked the room most of all because of the airplane propeller.

The propeller was huge. It took up an entire wall. Will knew from his grandfather's stories how the long, broad blades used to spin into a silver disk and blow air with hurricane force backward, through a tunnel inside the barn.

"Your Pa put that in for me," Grampa had told Will many times. "I told Josh, I said, 'I wished I had a way to dry out the wet hay.' And didn't he go out and get me an airplane propeller!"

Will never was sure if his grandfather was more amused or amazed by it, but telling the story, Grampa would start laughing. He'd laugh until his eyes watered and he had to wipe at them with the back of his hand. Grampa was proud of that propeller though. And proud of how Will's father had rigged it up for him.

Back in Baltimore Will's father made him the envy of the neighborhood by building a little car out of a lawn-mower motor and the wheels from two tricycles. The Willard Seymour they called it. (After Will, who was named for his grandfather.) The Willard ran on real gas and could putt-putt up and down the sidewalks through Patterson Park at five miles an hour.

"Josh by gosh," Grampa was always saying. There wasn't a kid Will knew who had a father like his. He used to feel so lucky.

Will stared at the floor. Sunlight, falling through a wide, open window, formed a golden square that shimmered and seemed to float before him. A magic carpet? Will never stopped hoping. Taking in a deep breath, he stepped onto it and closed his eyes.

At first, there was only silence, and the smell of hay dust and harness leather filling his nostrils. But then came the sound of laughter—children, laughing at him!

Startled, embarrassed, Will's eyes flew open. He rushed to the open window. "Hey!" he started to yell. But there were no kids. Just a barn-yard, long unused and now filled with tall grass and overgrown weeds.

Still, the sound came: faraway laughter and brief snatches of conversation. Odd how the sound kept popping out, like loose threads in the smooth, cool sheet of morning.

Frowning, his eyes skimmed the pasture and then the sky. Not children—but geese, Will realized. He could see them now. A large V of dark-colored birds winging high above the orchard. He leaned out the window on his elbows to get a better look and noticed how the fluid lines of the flock were rearranging themselves, forming, with grace, a different kind of V.

This would be a family heading south together, Will figured, to where it was warm, to where there was food for the winter. Watching them, Will filled with longing. Goose bumps prickled his arms. For the briefest moment, he imagined flipping the switch on the old propeller and letting the wind take him right out the window. He'd catch up with the flock if he could. Oh, to be a bird and fly away!

"Will?"

His hands clenched.

"Will, are you in here?"

Reluctantly, Will took his eyes off the flock. It was Grampa calling. His uneven steps made the loose wooden floorboards creak and echo in the empty barn.

"Answer me, son!"

His grandfather's voice, so close, suddenly touched a nerve in Will. "In the back, Grampa!" he responded.

Grampa came into the room with his hands on his hips. But Will could tell he wasn't really angry, just worried. "Will, we been looking all over for you. What's wrong?"

Will shrugged. "I don't know. Don't want to go, I guess."

"Aw, come on. It's a nice school. I checked it out for you last week." His grandfather came over and put an arm around his shoulders. "You got a right pretty teacher, too. Miss Ritter's her name." Grampa straightened up. "Excuse me, Will. Make that Ms. Ritter."

13

"You've got to look upon this as an adventure, Will. A whole new adventure!"

Sure, he thought to himself, it could be fun if he didn't have to worry so much. If everything else was normal, the way it was before his father lost his job.

His grandfather persisted. "It'll be okay. Take my word. The day'll go fast. Before you know it we'll be having us a lemonade and a game of checkers on the back porch."

Will let his grandfather steer him toward the doorway.

"Got a joke for ya, Will. Knock, knock."

Will sighed. He knew Grampa meant well. But sometimes, he wished his grandfather wouldn't try so hard.

"Come *on*. Knock, knock."

Halfheartedly, Will replied, "Who's there?"

"Ferdie."

"Ferdie who?" Will asked.

"Fer-die last time, cheer up!"

Will rolled his eyes, but he just had to smile.

2
The Optic Wonder

Back at the house, Will's mother was at the kitchen table trying to mix pancake batter. It was not an easy job with Will's two-year-old twin sisters standing on chairs to either side of her, each struggling for control of the long wooden spoon.

"Molly! Megan! You'll get a turn. Just wait a minute!" she said to them in a firm voice.

Will smiled and Grampa chuckled.

"Will! Where have you been?" his mother asked. "It's time for school."

She handed the spoon to Megan, which upset Molly immediately. "Me turn!" she whined. Will's mother shook her head as she grabbed a dishtowel and wiped her hands.

"I'll get Josh up. He needs to take Will to school."

"Don't bother, Miriam. I can take the boy," Grampa said. "Josh is still sleeping, isn't he?"

"He's asleep all right. You would be, too, if you got in at two o'clock in the morning." She threw the towel down on the table.

Grampa seemed surprised at her angry outburst. Will was not.

"I'm sorry," Will's mother said. "I didn't mean to snap. It's just that Josh said he wanted to take Will on his first day of school here and I think he should. I'll go get him."

Will felt his stomach start to knot up. He hoped this didn't lead to another argument.

When his father came into the kitchen tucking his T-shirt into his jeans, Will could see that his eyes were a little puffy. Will's mother was right behind him, her face without expression. Will knew she was unhappy, but at least she wasn't yelling. For the moment, Will was relieved.

His father rubbed his eyes with his fists and picked up his shoes by the door. "You all set, Will?" he asked as he sat on a kitchen chair.

"I guess so," Will answered.

Grampa squeezed his shoulder. "Don't you worry now. Everything is gonna be just fine. You'll see."

Will nodded glumly and let his mother give him a big hug. The little girls looked up at him, wide-eyed but silent, somehow sensing that this was Will's moment. "Good luck," his mother said. She brushed the hair out of his eyes. "I'll be thinking about you all day."

Will's father finished tying his shoes. "Let's go."

Seated high in his father's pickup truck, Will leaned forward and rolled down the window so he could wave good-bye to the girls. They looked cute, he thought, standing in the back door in their footed pajamas.

"Bye-bye, Wee!" Molly called out. Will smiled. "Wee" was as far as Molly had gotten in sounding out his name. Megan, on the other hand, had yet to speak her first word, let alone Will's name. One more thing the family worried about.

"Bye! Be good girls, okay?" Will called back. Something about their small, round faces suddenly made him feel more courageous about the morning ahead. The girls kept waving even as the truck jerked into first gear and pulled away.

Will's father yawned and ran one hand through his thick dark curls. They were the same dark curls Megan had. People were always saying Megan was her father's daughter. It made Will envious. He wanted to look like his father, too, but he and Molly with their straight, blond hair took after Will's mother.

"Boy! I've got to wake up here!" his father said suddenly, taking a deep breath. He eased the truck down Grampa's long, winding driveway, then turned onto the main road. Resting one arm out the window, he pressed his foot down on the accelerator. A little too hard, Will thought. His father didn't used to speed like this.

He glanced at his father again, but his eyes were hidden behind dark sunglasses.

"You don't need to rush, Dad. I don't think I'll be late."

His father didn't say anything, just kept driving, now with just one hand on the steering wheel.

"I'm sorry. Did you say something, Will?"

Will knew his father hated it whenever he was told to slow down or not be late, things like that. So he thought better of repeating himself.

"I said, 'What are you going to do today, Dad?'"

His father looked out his side window briefly. "Same thing I did yesterday, I guess. Go look for a job."

"Where?" Will asked, recalling that yesterday his father had unsuccessfully sought work at a lumberyard and then drove around in his truck until after everyone else had gone to bed.

"Well. I run into an old friend last night. Guy named Harding. Harding says he knows someone named Bob Wilson who might need help driving a moving van. I figured I'd go look up this guy, Wilson."

Will nodded. It seemed like a good idea to him.

"You know, that reminds me, Will," his father said. "I was telling Harding I had a son. He gave me something for you. Open the glove box."

Will leaned forward to push in the button. When the glove compartment popped open, a small box fell out. Will caught it in his hands.

"The Optic Wonder," he read. He tapped the open end of the box against his hand and a small black object fell into his palm.

"What's it do, Dad?"

His father shrugged. "All I know is Harding won three of 'em at the County Fair last week pitching dimes into an ashtray."

Will extracted a piece of paper from the box and smoothed it out on his lap. The paper crinkled beneath his hand. He began to read aloud: "The Optic Wonder is a unique optical instrument with multiple functions. It's a compass, a magnifying glass, a signal mirror..."

He paused to reshape the tool like one of his Transformers, popping out different lenses and flicking up tiny mirrors. "Neat!" he said, turning it into a magnifying glass.

He focused it back on the directions and continued reading aloud: "By opening both the large and small lens, the Optic Wonder becomes an adjustable binocular for viewing sports events as well as theater and—listen to this, Dad—opera!"

They look at each other and snorted because neither one of them could stand listening to opera. Will's mother loved it though. If Will's father was around when she had one of her tapes going, he'd sneak up to Will and whisper in his ear: "Hasn't that woman laid her egg yet?" It never failed to make Will laugh.

"Hey! I think we can put that Optic Wonder to better use watching third base at Camden Yards," his father said. "What do you think?"

Will hadn't thought of taking the Optic Wonder to an Orioles game. "Cool," he said.

"Say, lookee there," Will's father said leaning forward as he shot across a small bridge and sped down a road that ran between two open fields. "Looks like a flock of honkers. Just in time, too. Huntin' season opens tomorrow down in Maryland. Your Uncle Lester and I are gonna go bag us a couple."

"You are?"

His father nodded. "You betcha. Get your mother to cook us a roast goose."

"Can I go?" Will asked.

His father smiled, but didn't answer. He was still leaning forward, staring up at the geese while Will struggled to turn his Optic Wonder into a pair of binoculars so he could get a better look.

Neither one of them saw the doe and her fawn in the middle of the road up ahead.

"Whoa!" Will's father cried, swerving sharply to the right and hitting his brakes hard. The truck skidded sideways through soft sand on the edge of the road, then plunged forward down a small embankment, slamming into the bottom of a wet ditch.

The impact threw both Will and his father hard against their seat belts and back with a jolt against the seat.

"You all right, Will?" his father asked.

Will was okay, just scared. He nodded and rubbed the back of his neck. "What happened?"

"A deer," his father said. "Two of 'em. You didn't see?"

Will shook his head.

His father dropped his face into both hands and leaned into the steering wheel. "My God," he said. "I could've killed us both."

"It's all right, Dad. I'm okay."

His father kept his face buried, took a deep breath and let it out slowly into his hands.

"It's a good thing we had our seat belts on," Will said. "We'd have gone right through the windshield, I'm sure."

Slowly, his father sat up. "I was driving too fast, Will. Not looking. Not caring. I'm just not thinking!"

Will didn't argue. His father was driving too fast—way too fast.

"I don't know what's happening to me, Will. I feel like I'm losing it somehow. And I don't know where it's going to end."

Will struggled to understand. He knew that what his father was saying went beyond the truck running off the road. He knew that something else—something big—had been looming and growing for months over his family, the way a rolling, dark storm cloud builds end over end on a hot, stifling afternoon before it finally bursts.

But what was it exactly? What could Will say?

"I just don't know what to do," his father murmured.

Will wanted to help. He wanted to help more than anything else in the world. It's just that he felt sort of lost, too. His bottom lip began to quiver. Timidly, he reached across the front seat to touch his father's hand.

His father's hand was rough, but it felt good as he opened his thick, warm fingers and took Will's hand.

He looked up at his father. And when his father turned to him, Will could see that he was crying.

3

A Highway in the Sky

"Okay! When I tell you, ease off the clutch and slowly— SLOWLY—press your foot down on the accelerator. Got that?"

Will nodded. "Got it!" he hollered back.

His father stood in front of the left front wheel and was going to push the truck while Will backed it out of the ditch. Will had driven Grampa's small tractor before so he knew how to use a clutch. But he'd never driven his father's truck and he could barely reach the accelerator, never mind press down on it slowly. Still, it was exciting and he couldn't wait to try.

"Okay! Go ahead, Will!"

Will eased up on the clutch, stretched his right leg and pushed the ball of his foot against the pedal. The truck bucked once, then shot backward up the embankment. Will lost control of the accelerator altogether and the truck promptly stalled on the road with a jerk.

Will could feel his heart pounding.

"Good job!" his father called out.

Will heaved a sigh of relief and gladly slid back over to the passenger side.

When his father climbed into the driver's seat he was smiling. "All right!" he said, starting up the truck. He drove away carefully and slowly.

They were quiet the rest of the way, but in the school parking lot, his father reached over to muss up Will's hair. "Tell you what," he said. "On the way back, I'll stop at Driscoll's and get some bloodworms. When you get home from school we'll go up to the pond and do some fishing. What do you say?"

"That'd be great, Dad." He loved fishing with his father. Loved it as much as anything he could think of, except maybe going to a baseball game.

"Tell you what else," his father went on. "Maybe we'll even get the old Willard Seymour out of the garage and put in a new spark plug."

Will's mouth dropped. "I don't believe it. Is that what you think is wrong?"

His father nodded. "Yeah. I think that's all it is."

"I thought so! Didn't I say so?"

His father nodded.

"I can't wait. I can't wait to take that car all over the place at Grampa's!"

"Okay. You ready now?" He reached over to pick up Will's back-pack from the floor and handed it to him. "We've got to get you into this here school."

Will wrinkled his nose, but it was okay now."

In the main office at Blackstone Elementary School, Will shook hands with his father instead of hugging him like he wanted to and dutifully followed the secretary down the hall to Ms. Ritter's room.

His friend, Robbie, back in Baltimore, had warned him his new class would be filled with a bunch of dumb, country hicks. But at first glance, the kids in Ms. Ritter's class looked normal.

"Will, welcome to the fifth grade at Blackstone Elementary."

His teacher's voice was warm and sincere. She showed Will where to hang his backpack, "for the time being," she said, on a row of hooks in the back of the classroom. Then she indicated an empty desk in a cluster of four faced together. Will sat stiffly, pressing his back against the hard classroom chair.

"Will, this is Larry Praeger and this is Sarah Lacey," Ms. Ritter said, introducing the two children who would sit closest to him. The fourth desk was empty.

Will half-smiled at Larry and Sarah, then quickly dropped his eyes. He decided he would keep his distance here. If no one got close, then no one would have to know about his father and how he lost his job.

"We understand it's difficult entering a new school, Will," Ms Ritter said. "But don't be nervous. We'll try very hard to make you feel at home."

"Yes ma'am," Will said.

"Will is from Baltimore!" Ms. Ritter said much too cheerfully as she returned to her desk. "I'll bet he has some good city stories for us country bumpkins."

Deep inside, Will groaned.

The kids were staring at him. Will wondered if they were disappointed he didn't look more like a "city kid." Did they expect him to come in with chains on his belt? Or have an earring in his nose or something? The fact was, he didn't think a single solitary thing made him stand out. He wasn't skinny. He wasn't fat. He didn't wear glasses. He was just an ordinary kid, except for maybe his hair. Seemed like it was always in his eyes.

"Well. Perhaps we'd better get on with our science lesson," Ms. Ritter said.

Will relaxed, relieved to be out of the spotlight.

"Yesterday we started making a list of some of the changes taking place now, at the time of the autumnal equinox…"

Will snuck a quick look at the boy beside him. He had a bunch of curly red hair and a heap of freckles across his nose. Now there was a kid who stood out, Will thought.

"Because the earth is tilted, less sunlight hits the Northern Hemisphere," Ms. Ritter continued. "Shorter periods of daylight, remember? And that means what?"

The girl on the other side of Will raised her arm and shook it vigorously. He turned to watch her dark ponytail swing back and forth.

"Go ahead, Sarah," Ms. Ritter said.

"It means the leaves lose their green chlorophyll…"

Will's mind started to drift. He hoped his father was driving carefully back to the house, or to wherever he was going to talk about the moving van job.

Ms. Ritter wrote "Chlorophyll Degrades/Autumn Colors" on the blackboard. "What else?" she asked.

Will frowned, thinking back on the morning and wondering what it was that made his father drive so fast.

"What else?" Ms. Ritter asked again.

Someone said something and Ms. Ritter exclaimed, "Yes!" and wrote "Birds Migrate" on the board. Her excitement drew Will's attention.

"Isn't it wonderful to hear the Canada geese fly over?"

No one responded, but Will was remembering how his father leaned forward in the truck to get a better look at the geese—and then ran the truck off the road!

"Oh, come on," Ms. Ritter urged. "Don't you get excited when you hear those first geese come over? Doesn't that primal sound reach into your soul and give you shivers?"

When Ms. Ritter crossed both her hands over her heart, Will remembered the goose bumps he got watching the flock from the back of the barn that morning. Was it possible, he wondered, that the sound of geese had reached into his soul? He glanced at the boy beside him, who had lowered his head to giggle.

"People, *please*," Ms. Ritter implored. "I want you to take notice of these things and appreciate the beauty of the world around you! The sound of migrating geese should fill you with excitement and wonder and make you feel hopeful and happy about life renewing itself!"

As she walked briskly toward a big map at the front of the room the boy next to Will leaned over to whisper, "You should've seen her last week. She read a poem and started *crying*!"

The girl with the ponytail swung around. "She did not, Larry!" she hissed. "She had tears in her eyes, is all."

"It's called the Atlantic Flyway," Ms. Ritter said, "but I want you to think of a highway in the sky…"

Ms. Ritter tapped her bright red fingernails on northern Quebec and Will looked dreamily toward the window, his mind wandering back to the farm where he'd first seen the geese that morning. The smell of the hay dust and harness leather…He could still hear them, calling to each other, high above the orchard. A shimmering square of sunlight… Maybe, just maybe, Will thought, they were calling to him.

"If they have to, they can do it in just a couple of weeks," Ms. Ritter was telling the class. Will kept his eyes fixed on the blue sky out the window and began to wonder what it would be like for a young goose on its first migration, flying hundreds—*thousands*—of miles away to some unknown place. Would it know somehow that this trip was different? Would it be excited? Confused? Would it hesitate before it sprang into the air?

Or would it be just plain scared, and go along because it was part of the flock, because when you're young you don't have any say in the Big Decisions. Because sometimes, you just had to hold things inside and go along, no matter what else happened, if you wanted to survive.

Gray Feather lifts his bill into the cool, clear air of northern Quebec and waits, unmoving, for the signal. Nearby, a deep blue pond shimmers like a pool of diamonds in the autumn sunlight. Along its edges the geese continue to gather.

Hatched in the spring, Gray Feather is barely four months old and doesn't understand it all. But for days now, he and the other geese have been growing restless. From nowhere, it seems, comes the urge to arch his neck and stretch his wings toward the sky.

Outwardly, the world is changing, too. Even the daily balance of light and dark has shifted. The sun, rising later and setting earlier, leaves long, cool nights in its wake. The reed grass that fringes their pond has turned from green to brown. And there remains that slippery, silvery thing that glitters on the ground each morning.

Gray Feather's father honks loudly in order to be heard and Gray Feather knows the moment is close. Still the geese wait. When the sun is a full orange egg in the sky, the signal is given and they lift off in droves.

One after the other, honking all the way, they work their wings until, at the right height, each bird is settled, one behind the other, into its own pocket of air.

Far below, a river, like a snake, slithers across the earth, twisting and turning until it is swallowed by the huge watery belly of Hudson Bay.

Mightily, steadily now, Gray Feather strokes. Before him, his mother's tail feathers quiver in the rushing wind. Behind, his sister's beak presses forward. They fly in two lines that lead to a single front, like the wings of a bird that has no body.

Gray Feather knows now that they are on a long journey, to a new home and a new way of life. He searches for his father, but the gander is out of sight, at the front, leading the way with the older, wiser birds. Still, Gray Feather never stops looking for the arc of white feathers that spreads across his father's tail, pointing the way like a brilliant arrow in this dark smudge of geese against the sky.

4
Baltimore

On the bus after school, Will folded his arms over the backpack on his lap and stared out the window at the passing farms and fields.

He was relieved the first day was over. Grampa was right, of course; everything went fine. His teacher was nice. Real nice. She found an empty locker for him in the hallway. Will had never had a locker before. It had a secret, three-number combination: 9-17-38. And inside, there were two hooks and a shelf up top.

The kids at school seemed okay, too. They drank milk at lunch from little plastic bags. It was part of an experiment, Sarah Lacey told him, to see if plastic bags were more economical than cartons. She showed Will how to punch a hole in his milk bag with the sharp end of the short, narrow straw.

It was only after the bus dropped him off at the end of Grampa's long winding driveway that Will felt the knot in his stomach begin to tighten a little.

Through the trees, at the top of the hill, Will could see his grandfather's old farmhouse with its wide front porch and double stone chimneys. The house where Will's father grew up.

Will had always loved the first sight of the farm as his father shifted gears in the family car and started up the long driveway for a visit. His grandmother would always spot them coming and be there at the kitchen door wiping her hands on her apron and making a big fuss over Will and how much he had grown. And Grampa's dog, Maggie, would be whacking her big black tail against everybody and licking Will's hands.

It never was quite the same after Grandma—and Maggie—died, Will thought sadly. He still loved the house, and visiting Grampa. It's just that it felt wrong for his family to be calling it home.

In Baltimore, they lived in a red brick row house with three white stone steps out front. It looked like every other row house on the block and wasn't very big inside, but he had his own room and there was a basement big enough to hold a pool table. He and his dad played a lot of pool together. They went crabbing off the Hanover Street bridge. They drove into town to see the Orioles play and always sat in the upper deck behind third, cracking peanuts and keeping score together. Sometimes, Will's mother came with them and they'd all hold hands walking the warm, busy streets back to their car.

The Port of Baltimore wasn't very far away. Will's father was a longshoreman there. He operated a crane that unloaded containers from foreign ships. The containers looked like railroad cars without wheels. You couldn't tell from the outside, but Will knew because his father told him that the containers were filled with things like wine, Walkmans, and ceiling fans.

Will had always figured that, like his Dad, he would one day work on the docks. Now he knew he never would. Sure, he understood his father wasn't the only one to go; a lot of men lost their jobs when the port lost business to Hampton Roads in Virginia.

Still, the port had let them down. And things had changed.

It wasn't just the lack of money either. Baseball games and karate lessons after school weren't such a big deal, he had discovered. Something deeper, something far more important, had seeped out of their lives in the past year.

Will remembered the afternoon the Willard Seymour broke and he had to push it four blocks, uphill, all the way home.

"Can you fix it, Dad?" Will had asked.

His father was stretched out on the couch in front of a fan doing nothing, just watching a dumb game show on television—and he didn't even like game shows!

"I'll take a look after dinner, Will," he said in a tired voice.

His father usually had a theory about things. "Do you think it's the spark plug again?" Will wondered out loud as they sat down to eat.

"Don't know," his father mumbled. Will's father always had a big appetite even though he never seemed to put on weight. He could eat three hamburgers in one sitting! But that night he ate only half of a taco, then pushed his plate away. Didn't even set it on the counter, just got up and left. Will's mother stared after him, stunned, because both of the girls were crying in their high chairs when he walked out of the room.

His father never did take a look at the Willard Seymour. Will stopped asking about it. Today was the first time his father had mentioned the Willard in months.

About a year after his father lost his job, the house in Baltimore was sold at auction and Will's family didn't even get the money. It went to the bank. Will never quite understood, but that's when they moved to Grampa's.

Grampa said Will's father could help seed the fields—soybeans one year, corn the next—and that maybe he could pick up an odd job here and there. At the very least, Grampa said, they'd have a roof over their heads.

Halfway up the long driveway, will stopped because he was afraid. He could hear Molly's voice behind the house, her singsong chatter carrying lightly, happily, in the air. It was coming home and never knowing what to expect that frightened him.

Will turned to see if his father's pickup truck was in the tractor shed, where he always parked it at Grampa's. But the space was empty.

Inside, Will's body tightened up. His stomach became a hard ball.

So he and his father wouldn't go fishing after all.

The Willard wouldn't get its new spark plug.

It had happened again.

"It's only temporary," he remembered his mother saying as they packed bags and boxes for the move to Grampa's. "As soon as Dad finds work everything will be back to normal. You should be glad, Will, because we still have each other."

"Hmmph!" he grunted out loud. Feeling angry and frustrated, he kicked at a stone. Then he stared into the empty shed wondering where his father was this time and how long he would be gone. He stared until his eyes filled with tears and he had to wipe them away with his hand.

Suddenly, the breeze picked up, stirring the bright yellow leaves on a nearby oak. It was then that Will heard them again. Faraway laughter and snatches of conversation. In the distance, a flock of thirty, maybe forty geese, came into view. Loosely strung into a V shape, they formed a velvet black ripple against the iron gray sky.

Will let his backpack slide off onto one arm while his eyes remained on the flock. Ms. Ritter was right, he thought. There was something exciting about hearing the geese. Something that made him suck in his breath and feel hopeful about things deep down inside.

The honking drifted in and out with the breeze until the flock was directly overhead, their high-pitched goose calls loud and clear. Will watched as the leader dropped back and another goose took its place. He kept watching, until the long, wavering column of geese disappeared, its magnificent chorus muffled behind a curtain of gathering clouds.

A headwind buffets the flock. Gray Feather stretches his long neck forward and honks. He is next to last in the long, V-shaped column. Never has he flown so high.

When the wind slacks off Gray Feather dips his head. Far below and behind is the pond where he learned to swim, a tiny blue puddle in a huge, gray slate of land.

A cloud floats above and the geese pass in and out of shadow. Canada unfurls beneath him now, the flat open tundra extending as far as the eye can see. Caribou trails crisscross each other in all directions as though a huge wolverine has sharpened its claws over the barren, treeless ground.

They fly until their weary wings can fly no more and the order is given to descend to a field, near a small pond. Gray Feather extends his wings and cups the air, lowering himself to the ground.

Soon, other geese arrive, some in flocks so huge that the air hums with the sound of their wings and a flood of moving, broken shadows sweeps over the ground.

Darkness seeps into the sky, flooding it, turning it into a pool of black liquid speckled by tiny, glimmering water bugs.

While the geese sleep on the water, Gray Feather's father stands guard ashore. He is the sentinel tonight. Neck stretched tall, head cocked to the wind, the gander listens and watches for danger.

A rustle in the marsh grass startles the flock. It is only a possum come to drink, but Gray Feather has never seen a possum before and the ghostly white form, low to the ground, frightens him. Gray Feather searches the shoreline for his father but can't find him. He doesn't see that, keen-eyed and fearless, the gander remains an unmoving silhouette in the silver moonlight.

A breeze from out of the northwest picks up, rustling the leaves on a nearby tree. The geese gather noisily. Gray Feather's wings are weary. It is time to rest. But the sky is clear and the moon is full. He straightens his neck in anticipation and the signal is given.

Now, as he sails into the wide sea of darkness, the night air whistles in his ears. Far below, moonlight sparkles like stardust on the river and huge, black waves of shadows crash silently across the earth.

Swiftly, the birds settle into formation, moving their wings in time to a beat no other animal can hear. Inspired by the harmony of earth and sky, the geese call out, singing to the night world a song that only they know.

5
Hercules

If you stared at a star long enough, you could almost see its flames flickering: first orange, then white, then blue. It was amazing, Will thought, that there were fires so big you could see them from millions of miles away. He blinked without taking his right eye from the telescope lens.

Beside him, Grampa leaned back in the chair he had carried outside and pulled a pipe from his mouth. Tobacco smoke curled around his head and meandered toward Will. Will didn't mind. The smell of pipe tobacco reminded him of good things: winter holidays, big dinners, and Grampa, lighting his pipe before turning on the football game or placing the checkerboard on the hassock.

"I forget what constellations are out now," Will said, taking his eye from the lens.

The sky had cleared and it was a cool night, with a moon so full and bright that Will and his grandfather cast long, crisp shadows over the front lawn.

"Well, let's see now." Grampa leaned forward, a hand on each knee, and studied the night sky.

Will waited, letting the pipe smoke settle thickly around him. Funny, he thought, but if it wasn't Grampa smoking, he wasn't so sure he'd like the smell after all.

"Aries the Ram shows up in early fall," Grampa said. "And Hercules. You like Hercules. Remember, Will? He's got those four stars in his right arm, where he's raising a huge club."

"Oh, yeah. That's right." Will scanned the sky. But he didn't see anything that resembled an arm *or* a club.

"Cygnus the Swan should be there, too."

The thought of a swan reminded Will of the geese.

"You know what, Grampa? Ms. Ritter says the Canada geese have a highway in the sky."

Grampa nodded. "Indeed I do know that. A two-thousand-mile highway. Runs from the Ungava Peninsula of northern Quebec— goose country—and down across New York state where they pick up the Susquehanna. They follow the river all the way to the Chesapeake Bay."

"She showed us on a map—the Atlantic Flyway."

Grampa seemed pleased. "In fact," he said, "it's time they be flying over."

"I saw some today—twice. And Ms. Ritter told us we might even hear some at night."

"Oh, clear nights like this, Will, the moon lights their way! Right pretty way to travel, too, with moonlight sparkling on the Susquehanna. It would be sort of like following a road map with the route all lit up in glitter."

A sparkling map. Will liked the notion.

"Course you know why they fly in V formation, don't you, Will?"

Will tried to remember. "Because it's easier somehow. The one up front breaks a path?"

Grampa nodded. "Yeah, that's right. The leader has to push through the air and kind of creates a vacuum behind it and off to one side. Ever noticed how race cars get up right behind the lead car, but a little bit off to one side?"

Will nodded.

"They're takin' advantage of the same thing, like the geese."

"Wow. I didn't know the geese were so smart," Will said.

"Smart? Hey!" Grampa went on. "You know why one side of the V is most always longer than the other side?"

Shaking his head slowly, Will said, "No, I give up."

Grampa grinned. "'Cause there's more geese on that side!"

Will started to laugh, then crossed his arms and leaned back in the chair. Grampa was always sneaking up on him with jokes like that. He turned his gaze skyward again, thinking about the geese in V formation making a path through the air.

"Do they ever stop, Grampa?" he asked. "Or do they fly straight on through, all the way to Maryland?"

"They stop all right. Stop right on this farm sometimes. Use my pond for a rest area, they do. I don't have any Coke machines but I do plant a field of corn for 'em." He pointed with his pipe. "Up there near the hemlock grove."

Will knew exactly which field he meant. Every year, Grampa cut it down and let it lie, unharvested. That would explain why he saw the geese flying behind the barn that morning. They were probably on their way to that field—or Grampa's pond.

"I figure that's my reparation, Will."

He turned to his grandfather. "Repar-ation?"

Grampa stroked his long white mustache with one hand and sighed. "Yeah," he said with a vague smile. "To make amends and give back some, for all the geese I've taken, hunting over the years."

There was a pause and Grampa added, "Good Lord says you shouldn't take, unless you's willing to give back some, too."

Will studied the sad, faraway look in his grandfather's eyes. He'd seen the look before and knew to respect it. Like the time Grampa took him over to the Gettysburg battlefield and walked him out into the middle of a cow pasture studded with gray boulders. "Your great, great grandfather Hezekiah Newcomb died here," Grampa had told him in a voice so solemn—so laden with emotion—that Will was afraid to look at his feet for fear there'd still be blood from the Civil War soaking through the ground.

Just then the kitchen door opened and they both turned. Will could see the profile of his mother's face and the way she had her long hair pulled back and knew she was looking off down the driveway.

"Guess we'd better go ahead and eat," she said. "I don't know where Josh is, but it's getting late. The girls are hungry and I'm sure you two are."

"Seems to me he said he was going down to Bob Wilson's to check on that truck driving job," Grampa recalled. "But that shouldn't have taken him this long. You think we ought to start worrying?"

Will's mother shrugged. "I have no idea," she said. She waited in the doorway for a moment, then quietly retreated, letting the door close softly behind her.

Grampa's thick white eyebrows knit together as he set a heavy hand on Will's shoulder. "Come on," he urged gently. "Let's eat. We can come back out later."

Inside, Will's mother lifted the twins into their booster seats while Grampa poured their milk. Will pitched in by tying bibs on the two girls. Molly, who was always wiggling and making noise, was singing "Yankee Doodle" to the tune of "Mary Had a Little Lamb."

Megan watched her twin sister with wide, amused eyes, but made no sound of her own.

"I see your Ma's cooked us one of those fancy New England dinners," Grampa remarked.

Will smiled because it wasn't fancy at all—just hot dogs, baked beans and steamed brown bread from a can. Grampa, for some reason, liked to tease Will's mother about her growing up in Boston.

"Do you have any homework this weekend?" Will's mother asked.

Will nodded. "I'm supposed to read as much as I can from a book Ms. Ritter gave me. We're doing book reports on Monday."

"Well, don't forget," his mother said. "You should start tonight so you don't have a hundred pages to read Sunday night."

Dinner was over by the time they heard a motor and saw head-lights through the kitchen window. By then, the girls had gone off to play and Will was clearing the last dirty plate from the table. He sat beside Grampa, and no one spoke until the door opened and Will's father walked in.

"Sorry I'm late, Miriam," Will's father said.

"You could have called," she replied without turning around. Dishes rattled in the sink.

"I guess I forgot. See, I went to see Bob Wilson about that truck driving job. He told me to meet him at The Riverside Café."

Will's mother didn't respond, just kept washing the dishes.

His father sighed and pulled out a kitchen chair. Will waited, wondering if he was going to remember his broken promise to go fishing and to fix the Willard.

"So what did Bob say?" Grampa asked.

Will's father looked at him. "He never showed up."

Grampa winced.

A long moment passed when no one said anything. Will felt sorry for his father. He was glad he hadn't told his mother or Grampa about the accident they had that morning.

"So," his father finally said. "How was school, Will?"

"Great," he said flatly. He knew his father wasn't really listening because he was looking at Will's mother.

"Miriam, I'll watch the kids tonight if you want to just get out for awhile, go shop or something."

"Go shop?" She turned. "With what? We don't have any money, remember?"

His father slowly folded his hands on the table and stared at them.

"I'm sorry," Will's mother said. "I know you're disappointed. Once again. But Josh, you could have called us. We had no idea where you were!"

"Yeah," he sighed. "I suppose. I was just so bummed out I went and sat by the river. Lost track of time, I guess."

"You can't just go disappear for half a day! It's not right, Josh. You've got to get hold of yourself."

Will could feel the argument coming. His mother did this all the time now. As soon as his father got home, she was nice. "How are you?

What happened? You hungry?" she'd ask. Then he'd say something and she'd jump on him for something else and they ended up fighting! His mother didn't used to be this way. His parents used to hug each other when Will's father came home from work. They used to laugh and tell stories and repeat things Will and his sisters had done.

Not anymore.

Will looked over at Grampa who was filling his pipe with tobacco and staying out of this one.

"Miriam, I—"

"Well, how do you think we feel?" she snapped, cutting him off.

Will couldn't stand it. "Dad!" he blurted out, interrupting. "Can I go hunting with you tomorrow?"

"Hunting? You're going hunting?" Will's mother asked.

Will gulped.

"Miriam, every fall I go hunting with my brother."

"Don't you think things are a little different this year?" she asked.

Will's father shrugged. "Couple nights and it's not going to cost anything. I stay with Lester. It's not like I have a job to get back to, you know?"

"Dad! Can I go? Please, can I go this time?"

His father seemed distracted. "I don't think so, Will."

"But I've never been. And I've always wanted to."

"No—"

"I could help you with the dogs!"

His father shook his head.

Will turned to his mother, who was slowly wiping her hands on a dishtowel. He figured she was really going to explode and braced himself for the attack.

She surprised everyone. "Why not?" she asked, her voice soft, questioning. "If you're going hunting, why not take Will with you? It would be good for you two to do something together. You haven't had any fun like that for months."

Will's eyes widened in disbelief.

A puff of smoke rose from across the table. "Sounds like a good idea to me," Grampa said.

"But Will's never handled a shotgun. I mean, gee, Pop, he's only ten—"

"Eleven!" Will reminded him.

"Whatever. Eleven."

Grampa's eyebrows rose. "Josh, you were eight years old the first time you went goose huntin' with me!"

"Yeah, but a kid's got to be twelve years old now to hunt."

"In Pennsylvania, maybe. There's no age limit in Maryland. That's where you're going, isn't it? Down to Lester's?"

"But he's still got to pass a hunter safety course."

Grampa waved a hand at him, disgusted. "You can teach him what he needs to know."

Josh leaned over the table and looked his father in the eye. "It's the law, Pop. Law says you got to pass this course."

"Yeah? Well, I taught *you* everything *you* know about huntin'!"

"That was a long time ago," Will's father dropped his eyes.

"Look at me!" Grampa ordered. "Don't you remember paddling around in that old mud scow setting out the floaters? There wasn't a decoy out of place in that pond."

"But that was different—"

"It weren't no different then! A boy's a boy! You loved being out there the same way Will would. And you can teach him what he needs to know."

Will's father was not convinced. Will could tell.

"Sure," Josh said after awhile. "And then what if he gets bored? And cold? It's miserable in those goose pits. He's not used to it."

Grampa pointed his pipe at Will's father. "Josh Newcomb, you loved every *miserable* minute you spent down in that pit, talking to the dogs, eatin' donuts, pokin' your head up through the switchgrass to see if them honkers was coming in yet. You was always the first to see—you and Lester's dog, Lady."

Will's father stared at the floor, his face softening with the memories.

Grampa grinned. "She was some dog, wasn't she, Josh?"

A whole family tree of black Labradors had rooted and branched out during Grampa's lifetime. Will knew from the stories, told many times over, that Lady was a purebred champion hunting dog that Uncle Lester had won as a puppy. She was "best of the best," Grampa always said. She was also mother to many other Labrador retrievers, including a dog named Lucy Mae, who was the mother of Grampa's beloved Maggie.

"Lady would break ice to get a downed goose if she had to," Grampa said, shaking his head. "Never could get my Maggie to retrieve with the same fire in her belly."

If anyone could get his father to change his mind it was Grampa.

"But Lester's not going to want Will along, Pop."

Grampa scoffed. "Lester don't care! He raised three boys of his own!"

Will's father spread his hands out on the table. "I guess the truth is, I—well, I just wanted to go by myself."

"Yourself!" Will's mother came forward, grabbed the back of a kitchen chair. "You're by yourself all the time, Josh. You never do anything with Will anymore!"

Will's father scraped back his chair and stood up. "Do something with Will? I'm supposed to be finding work, Miriam! I have a family to support, remember?"

"Of course, I remember—"

"Well, get off my back then!" he hollered.

"I'm not on your back!"

"You are on my back! You're on my back all the time, for cryin' out loud!"

"I am trying to hold this family together, Josh! It needs more than a paycheck, you know!"

"Yeah, yeah, sure."

"You're not listening to what I'm saying, Josh."

"No, I'm not because I'm sick of what I'm hearing!"

With that, Will's father shoved the chair aside and walked out of the room.

Will's mother followed.

Inside, Will felt flat, the way you feel when you lose at something so many times it doesn't hurt anymore.

"You can't keep walking away from everything," his mother said in the other room.

"Don't push me, Miriam. I'm warning you. Don't push me."

Will couldn't stand it anymore. When the girls started crying, he fled up the back stairs that led from the kitchen to the second floor. In the bedroom he shared with his sisters he shut the door and threw himself across the foot of his bed.

Through the window a tiny, red light appeared in the night sky. An airplane? Will covered his ears, trying, unsuccessfully, to block out the shouting downstairs. He had never been in an airplane. His father used to say they would all fly to Disney World one day, but he knew they never would now.

Downstairs, the kitchen door slammed and Will stiffened, knowing he would next hear the motor of his father's pickup truck turn over. His chest tightened. He never used to think this way, but now, every time his father left, he wondered deep in his heart, if it might be for good.

He still had his hands over his ears when his grandfather came into the room. The smell of his pipe smoke preceded him.

Grampa sat on the edge of his bed. "You know, Will," he began, "You're not going to believe this, but your father does love you."

Will took his hands off his ears and grunted. "Sure."

"You Pa is so wrapped up in his own troubles right now he can't tell his right hand from his left."

"But I don't get it. Why is it better to be alone?"

Grampa shook his head. "I don't know, Will. Sometimes people got to go off and figure things out for themselves. Your Pa never was good at listening to people. He certainly hated to listen to me—no matter what I had to say."

Frowning, Will settled back down with his chin on his hands and stared out the window.

"Even as a boy, your Pa had to do everything himself, the way he saw fit," Grampa went on. "Some people, I guess, that's the only way they know how."

Grampa sat there for a long while. Finally, he patted Will on the back of his leg and stood up to go. "He loves you, son. We all love you," he said.

The tiny red light was gone. When the door clicked shut behind his grandfather, Will renewed his search for the four stars that formed Hercules' right arm.

$\mathcal{G}$ray Feather and the others in his flock fly as fast as they can but a single, red eye blinks in the night, pursuing them with frightening speed. It roars and the sound is deafening. Like thunder breaking over their heads, it surrounds them.

Suddenly, and all at once, they cup the air with their wings and descend, before the airplane is upon them.

Sticking out his feet, Gray Feather settles with a gentle thud and a short run on smooth, cool grass. As he tucks in his wings, he casts a glance back at the sky, but the unseen enemy is gone and the roar grows fainter and fades away, like the distant rumble of a thunderstorm that has passed.

A gentle rain begins. Together, the geese move like a giant, undulating insect, down a grassy hillside to a pond for a long, cool drink.

All night the rain continues, harder at times, in heavy sheets that batter the treetops and soak the ground. Gray Feather tries to sleep but cannot. So he stands beneath the hardwoods and uses the time to calmly preen himself, jabbing his beak at the oil gland near his tail and spreading the oil amongst his feathers to keep them dry.

A tiny beetle scurries by. Gray Feather nabs it with lightening speed and swallows.

Just before dawn, when the rain finally lets up, Gray Feather is the first to step out of the woods and make his way back to the pond. With some of the younger geese he swims off toward a patch of wild rice where they take turns tipping to nibble at the underwater roots.

Gray Feather's father stands on the bank watching the youngsters. Gray Feather honks, but it is not the sound of alarm or fear. The sun tries to poke through the dark clouds. Excited, eager to fly again, he whips the water with his wings and noisily lifts off from the creek. The others trail behind him in a loose and ragged V formation.

A light drizzle tickles their faces. Warning calls are issued from the elders gathered below, but the young geese follow Gray Feather over the wet and glistening forest, through banks of fog so heavy a goose can barely see a wingspan ahead.

Far below, the landscape changes. Strange bugs hustle along

straight stone paths, sparkling, whenever a rare sun ray hits them, making them look like flecks of silver in a granite rock.

Suddenly, the sun is gone completely and the wind picks up. Flying becomes a struggle. Gray Feather has no one to cut a path for him. He turns back but the wind blows them all out of formation and drives hard, stinging pieces of frozen rain against them.

Now, chunks of ice, thick as hickory nuts, pelt the geese from all sides. Gray Feather flails in the air. He honks for his father and tries to land but the ice hammers at him until he crumples and drops, alone, like a falling star hurtling through space.

6
A Dirty Trick

Will awoke with a start. But why? A bad dream? It was still dark and Will could hear it raining, a light but steady patter that pinged against the metal gutters outside his window and kept time with his thumping heart. He shivered and snuggled deeper beneath his quilt.

When he was a little boy and a nightmare made him call out in the night, his mother would tuck him back in with a soft kiss on the forehead and tell him to think of something happy, like picking up shells at the beach.

So he thought about the day he and his father went to see their first baseball game in the new stadium at Camden Yards. His father bought him an Orioles cap, the one he still wears, and afterward they rode the light rail train all the way down to Glen Burnie and back, just to see what it was like.

Slowly, Will realized it was Saturday. He was relieved he didn't have to go to school. He felt himself drifting again, until the wood floor in the hallway creaked and Grampa poked his head in.

"Are you coming with me or not?" he asked.

Will sat up, confused. "Where you going?"

"Shhh," Grampa held a finger to his lips and nodded toward the far wall where Molly and Megan lay asleep in their cribs.

"Goin' huntin'."

"Are you kidding?"

Grampa pointed to himself. "Would I kid you?"

Will whipped off his covers. By the time he was dressed and

downstairs in the kitchen, Grampa already had a fire going in the wood stove and was pouring coffee into a thermos.

"We're going hunting, Grampa?"

He nodded.

"But I thought you had to be twelve years old to hunt in Pennsylvania?"

Grampa grunted and screwed the top on his thermos. "Let's not get into that again. There's probably a lot of ten year olds in this state that are far more qualified to handle a gun than some of the forty-year-old fruitcakes I seen out there."

Will was doubtful. "But don't you still need a license or something?"

"Nope. Farmers who work their land don't need one. Just got to update my duck stamps every year and I do that religiously. Every fall, I go down the post office to get my stamp, sign it, stick it in my wallet. Even if I don't hunt no more, I still get one."

"So." Will smiled a little. "I guess we're going hunting then. But how come so early?"

Best time to get geese is early morning or just before the sun sets. That's when they're likely to be moving around. Will. "Sides that though, I want to get out before your folks get up and throw a fuss."

"Is Dad back?"

"Late last night. Everything's fine. Here, take these," Grampa thrust two packages of cupcakes at Will. "Push 'em in your pockets somewhere. There's not really time for breakfast."

Amused, Will picked up his jacket and shoved the cupcakes into its two front pockets.

"That hold you for awhile?" Grampa asked.

Will nodded. "But I still don't get it."

"We're going to show your Pa you're boy enough to get a goose. Then maybe he'll change his mind about not taking you with him to Lester's later today."

Grampa seemed determined as he zipped open an ancient, Army knapsack and stuffed in the morning's supplies: a box of shotgun shells, two cans of soda, the thermos, a First-Aid kit. "Guess we got to *show* him something. Can't ever seem to *tell* him anything," he grumbled. Will still wasn't sure what to think. He had to chuckle though, when his grandfather pulled a bulky camouflage jacket over his overalls. The jacket was so big it made him look like Hulk Hogan. And his rumpled old fishing hat, sitting low on his half-bald head, forced tufts of white hair to stick out around his ears like a clown's.

Grampa put on his boots and ordered Will to do the same. Then he reached above the wood stove and carefully lifted his shotgun from a wooden rack.

"Wow. I've never seen you take it down, Grampa."

"I haven't used this Winchester in a long time, Will. But last night, after you were in bed, I cleaned it up."

He patted the wooden stock of his gun and Will could see that it had been freshly oiled, the long black double barrel rubbed until it shone. The gun was not the only thing glowing. Grampa's face had lit up as well. The little smile beneath his white mustache, the spark in his tired, red-rimmed eyes. This was really making him happy, Will realized. It was bringing back some pretty special memories.

Outside, the rain had left behind an eerie gray mist. As Grampa set off across the driveway the metal fasteners on his old boots jangled, the only sound in the quiet morning air. Will and three hungry cats followed close behind.

"Where we going now?" Will asked.

"You'll see," Grampa said, leading Will through the barn past the long row of iron stanchions where the cows used to stand for their daily milkings. He was a little boy when his grandfather retired from dairy farming, but Will still remembered the big black-and-white Holsteins with their wide, wet noses and their steaming manure piles.

From his summer visits, Will had come to know all of the barn's special places: the hayloft, the milk room with the its huge stainless steel cooler, and way in the back, the feed room, which they entered.

Here, grain for the cows used to be stored in burlap sacks on long, wooden pallets before being dumped into a deep, rectangular bin, which Will always thought looked like a huge toy chest.

His grandfather set the shotgun down, pointing it away from them, and lifted the top of the grain bin filling the air with reminders of the rich, molasses-soaked feed.

"Can't go huntin' without our decoys," he said, reaching in to pull out a large canvas bag. The bag clunked noisily as it was lowered to the floor. Dust filled the air and the cats scattered.

Grampa pulled open the top of the bag so Will could peek in at the wide-eyed wooden geese inside. "Gee. I never knew these were here," he said, feeling somewhat cheated. All these years and he never once thought to open the bin.

They loaded the decoys into an old wagon, which Will pulled through the pasture. As it bumped along, the wagon's rusty wheels protested noisily. Annoyed, a crow squawked overhead and disappeared into the nearby woods.

The sun was coming up and the sky was clearing. Beads of moisture sparkled on the grass and patches of fog lifted from the soggy earth like wisps of steam over a cup of tea.

"Looks like we had some hail last night," Grampa said.

"How can you tell?"

"A lot of little branches broken. Grass beaten down."

Will started to say that he had heard the hail but then shrugged, wondering if he'd dreamed it instead.

They trudged on, eventually following an old cow path that wound its way sideways, back and forth, up a steep hill half-covered with prickly juniper bushes. At the top they stopped to rest.

Grampa took off his hat while he caught his breath. "Pretty, ain't it, Will?" he said, wiping his forehead with the back of his hand.

Will nodded. It was truly beautiful in all directions: the farm behind them, the pond below in the tree-shaded hollow. Without a word, they stood side by side looking south, over fields of corn and soybeans so neatly parceled in squares of yellow, brown and green that they covered the land like a huge, earthy quilt. In the distance, the Susquehanna River threaded its quiet, haphazard way through the countryside, a magnificent blue ribbon binding the rough patchwork of crops.

"Well!" Grampa said, plopping the hat back on his head. "Where'd you and your Pa stash that dinghy?"

Will jumped to his feet and ran downhill to the overturned rowboat. It was hidden behind boulders near the edge of the pond. In summers past, Will and his father had used the boat for fishing.

It took the strength of both of them to haul the boat down to the water's edge.

"Whew! I've got to rest a minute," Grampa said, sitting nearby on the trunk of a fallen tree.

Will took over and pulled the decoys out of the bag. Their chains and anchors rattled as he untangled them and carefully set each one in the boat. Will thought it interesting that each decoy was different. Some had straight necks as though alert, some had bent heads, as though feeding. Still others faced backward, their long necks resting upon their backs.

"How come they're not the same, Gampa?"

"You want it to look like a real flock, don't you? Geese are smart critters. If you had three dozen decoys with their necks straight up, the geese overhead would know something *else* was up!"

That made sense, Will decided. He clambered into the boat, settling himself among the silent, wooden flock.

Meanwhile, Grampa wet his index finger and stuck it up into the air.

"Wind's comin' from out of the south so that's the direction you want to face most of your decoys," he said. "Not all, but most."

Will frowned.

"Geese always land into the wind, Will. Take off the same way, too—like an airplane. That way, they get the most lift. But they feed into the wind, too. So they can take off fast if they have to."

"Huh. I didn't know that," Will said. He started to row out into the pond.

"Make sure now that your sentinel is one of the one's facin' the wind. The big guy!" Grampa called after him.

Will paused with the oars at rest and picked up the decoy with the longest, straightest neck. "This one?"

"That's the one!" Grampa gave him a thumbs up.

With his grandfather hollering yet more instructions from shore, Will set out the floaters, spacing them apart just enough so they looked like a real flock of geese.

When the last one was finally bobbing on the water, he rowed back to shore. Grampa popped open a can of soda for him.

"Now, pay attention, Will," he said. "First, I'm going to show you how to load this gun."

Will watched intently as his grandfather pressed a button near the middle of the gun and then easily bent the shotgun open. "Called breaking it open," Grampa said. "I'm going to slide one shell into each of the two barrels." When he finished, he snapped the gun shut.

"Now I'm going to show you how to get this gun into firing position."

Again, Will watched intently as his grandfather lifted the gun shoulder level.

"Weight on your left foot. Feet about twelve inches apart."

Will nodded.

"You want to press the stock into your shoulder. Then rest your cheek against it and cradle the barrels in your left hand, thisaway," Grampa said, demonstrating.

"Steady now, you look down the barrels until you see a little round bead at the end. You want to aim that bead about a foot in front of the goose's head."

"But don't shoot!" Grampa said, turning to Will. "Not until you see his eyes!"

"Okay," Will agreed. He put his soda on a flat rock nearby and reached for the gun.

But for a long moment, Grampa held his aim at the sky, as though enjoying the familiar stance. When he finally brought the gun down he looked hard at Will. "There's one thing you have to promise me, son," he said.

Will dropped his arms. "Sure. What is it, Grampa?"

His grandfather pointed to the little button off to one side of the trigger. "Don't ever press the safety to release the trigger until you're ready to shoot."

Again, Will nodded.

"That means the safety is never off before that gun is up to your shoulder."

"Yes, sir," Will acknowledged soberly.

At last, his grandfather relinquished the shotgun, which Will eagerly took into his own hands. It was the first time he'd ever held a shotgun and it surprised him that the gun was so heavy. He had to concentrate on not dropping it.

"Aim it at the top of the tree over there," Grampa ordered.

Mustering his strength, Will hoisted the big Winchester to his shoulder and cradled the long barrels with his left hand. He had to stretch his index finger just to reach the trigger.

"That's a boy. Good," Grampa said.

The feeling of having so much power at the tip of his finger was at once exhilarating and unsettling. When a small brown bird darted into view Will panicked and quickly lowered the gun. He couldn't imagine actually pulling the trigger and blasting the little bird out of the sky.

Grampa didn't notice. "Well. There's no goose blind anymore. Guess that's been gone about two decades." He nodded toward the bushes nearby. "We'll have to hide out over there."

All morning, Will tried not to think about the killing part. But now his mind kept going back to it, like a tongue to a sore tooth. Of course, Will thought, he'd probably be such a bad shot he'd never hit anything. But then, what would there be to show his father? Wasn't that the point?

Together, they sat on a log beneath a canopy of overgrown juniper bushes. Not long afterward they heard some geese. The birds were far away, mere pepper specks in the sky, their honking a light sprinkle of noise. Still it was enough to arouse the same excitement and when the sound drifted away, Will and Grampa stood listening anyway.

"What is it about hearing the geese, Grampa?" Will whispered. "What is it that makes you have to stop and listen?"

Grampa smiled and shook his head. "Gosh, Will. I don't know. But there is something to it, ain't there? I once heard someone, a newspaperman, talk about it on the radio. He said hearin' the geese in the fall was like hearin' an old song on the radio. It brings back memories to you. "Cepting the honking of the geese harkens aback to real ancient times when geese flying overhead meant a good meal was in store."

"Huh," Will said, thinking on that.

"A right pretty sound," Grampa went on. "Guess you never heard the geese living in Baltimore, did you?"

Will shook his head. There was nothing special, like the sound of geese, in the air over Baltimore. Just the busy clamor of machinery at the port, sirens wailing day and night, and whistle blasts from the ships coming up the Patapsco.

But that reminded Will of something and he brightened. "There was one thing, Grampa," he said. "If you rode by the Domino Sugar plant when the sugar ship was in, the air smelled sweet."

Grampa smiled. "Say now, that was special," he said.

Will checked the sky again. He was relieved the geese hadn't come any closer. He realized then that he didn't want to kill a beautiful Canada goose.

But he didn't want to look like a sissy either.

"Seems to me I had a goose whistle in here somewhere," Grampa grumbled as he rummaged through the knapsack. "Sure would help to call them in. A goose can't resist the call of another goose, Will."

For something to do, Will pulled out the Optic Wonder and checked the decoys. From where they sat, you couldn't tell they were pieces of wood, he thought. If he were a goose, he'd certainly fly in to see who was who. Focusing again, he noticed how, when the wind blew, the decoys pulled against their chains and bobbed in the water. It looked just like geese swimming.

He lowered the Optic Wonder and folded it back into itself. He was thinking that hunting could be a lot of fun if you didn't have to go and kill anything. As it was, the whole adventure was beginning to seem like a dirty trick.

He stood, pushing his hands in his pockets, and stared at the pond. "Doesn't it ever bother you, Grampa?" he asked. "I mean, shooting a goose and seeing it die and all?"

But Grampa had found a comfortable position on the ground, leaning back against the log with his eyes closed, his face turned up toward the sun, and didn't hear. Will sighed. It was just as well, he thought. Better not to make a big deal out of it. Not if he wanted to go hunting with his father. In the end, that was more important than a bird. Wasn't it?

Will kept thinking that if he and his father went hunting together, things would be better. It was a long ride to Uncle Lester's—two hours or more from here to the Eastern Shore of Maryland where his uncle lived and where they would hunt on his field. In the truck on the way over, he and his Dad could play that game: *I see something that begins with "h"*....His father always found really tough ones. They could tell jokes. They could sing that song real loud: *There was an old woman who swallowed a fly. But I don't know why she swallowed a fly*.... At Uncle Lester's they would sleep together on the pullout sofa in the living room and eat Aunt Phoebe's crab cakes with fried eggs for breakfast. Uncle Lester would have his father and him laughing about something until their sides ached.

All they needed was some time together. This could be the perfect chance.

Will sat back down on the ground beside Grampa and leaned his head against the log. As the morning wore on, he found himself wishing the geese *would* come so he could just shoot and get it over with.

The flock gathers, restlessly, at the bottom of a gentle slope. Water from the storm that has passed still rushes downhill carving deep, muddy rivulets in the spongy earth. A soft wind carries the scent of damp tree bark and wet grass. But the sky is a clear, pale blue now, the welcome color of a tundra blossom in early spring.

The flock is one less now. A female goose stands quietly on the muddy hillside, letting a shallow pool form around her feet. Her brown eyes watch the sky.

Suddenly, they can wait no longer. In a burst of movement, the geese are airborne and once again, the air hums with the sound of honking and wings.

Gray Feather's mother hesitates, but the call of one goose to another is strong. The bond within the flock cannot be broken. She, too, jumps into the air, following, with the others, the invisible pathway south.

7
A Bluebird Day

Grampa stirred and stretched his long arms. "You know, when I was a young'un I could call in a whole flock by myself."

Will yawned and sat up. "Do it then!" he said.

The old man chuckled. "Now that's a talent you gotta keep after, Will. Like playin' the piano."

Will smiled, imagining how his grandfather would look sitting in the bushes with his hands cupped around his mouth, honking like a goose. He tried it himself a few times, and got Grampa laughing.

By midmorning, they shed their jackets and broke out the cupcakes. Grampa poured himself black coffee from the thermos and they talked about a lot of things: school, the move from Baltimore— even Will's father.

"You've got to understand," Grampa said. "Your Pa's been going through a real hard time being out of work. It's kind of like losing your identity, not having a job. It would be like somebody taking my farm away from me.

"Your Pa's tried hard to get work, Will, and he's had to deal with a lot of rejection. He probably feels downright worthless at times."

Will picked up a stick and broke it in half.

"It's tough," Grampa went on, "to give back to a family when you're feeling so low. People like your Pa, Will, sometimes they're so depressed about the big picture in life that they lose sight of the day-to-day stuff, the little things that, when you come right down to it, mean the most."

Will poked one of the sticks into the ground. He remembered his father's sad face the morning the truck ran off the road. And then how his father went and forgot about fishing and the new spark plug for the Willard.

Grampa stood to check the sky again. "Looks like we're gonna have us a bluebird day."

Shading his eyes with one hand, Will peered up at him. "A bluebird day?"

"Means we get a great day—but no geese. Gray sky, a lot of low clouds, that's what geese like. Gives them plenty of places to hide while they're flyin'. I tell you, Will, those birds are smart critters."

Grampa crossed his arms. "Some of the best times I've had were days like this though. Just being outdoors, away from work, away from hassles. A couple of good friends—better yet, a couple of good dogs." Grampa smiled, remembering. "No, it never disappointed me to go home without a goose. Especially on a day like this."

Will started to peel the bark off his stick. "Grampa," he said, "I keep wondering about something."

"Yeah?"

"I just wondered if it…well, if it ever bothered you about shooting a goose. I mean, the killing of it."

His grandfather thought for a moment. "Didn't used to," he said. "You see, Will, I ain't never shot anything I didn't take home and eat. And I do believe in the laws of nature. If hunters stopped shooting altogether, coyotes and 'coons would be eating all the bird eggs. Deer would overpopulate and starve to death in the winter…"

Will looked up, waiting for the other half of the answer.

"A good hunter loves the land," Grampa went on. "He respects nature. I see it from both sides, Will."

"But if it never bothered you to shoot a goose, then why did you plant a whole cornfield for them?" Will asked. "Remember what you said? Your reputation?"

Grampa chuckled. "Reparation."

"Well?"

The old man shook his head. "Whew! You sure do make it hard, Will."

"Then you must've felt a little guilty, right? Something about it bothers you now."

Grampa didn't answer. He was distracted.

"Grampa! Is it geese?" Will dropped the stick and stood up.

"Shhhhhh. You don't want to scare'em off."

The honking drew closer, clarifying itself. Slowly, stealthily, Grampa and Will peeked over the bushes to see a long dark column heading their way.

As Grampa picked up the gun, which lay on the gound nearby, Will felt the old knot form in his stomach.

"You shoot first, Grampa," Will suggested.

"No," he answered firmly. "Take the gun."

As Will took it he noticed that Grampa's hands were shaking. "You okay?" he asked.

Grampa nodded.

The honking grew louder. Will turned to watch the geese as they began to lower themselves on a direct line to the decoys. Sure enough they were landing into the wind, too.

Lightly, Grampa touched Will's elbow. For the second time that day, Will lifted the heavy gun to his shoulder and cradled the long barrels with his left hand. They felt colder this time, like ice against the warm, sweaty flesh of his hand. Inside, the knot tightened. Despite what his body was saying, he had to get a goose. Carefully, he took aim.

"Pick out one on the outer flanks, now, toward the rear," Grampa whispered in his ear. "Don't take the leader. The older, wiser birds are up front. You don't want to deprive the flock."

Legs dangling, wings outstretched, the geese were almost directly in front of him now. A shiver ran through his body and all at once the gun seemed unbearably heavy. Will knew he wouldn't be able to hold it up much longer. His finger stiffened as it reached for the trigger. The polished wood of the stock pressed against his cheek so hard it hurt his teeth. Holding his breath, he drew a bead on a bird toward the rear and followed it down, down, down.

He could hear his grandfather breathing hard behind him and wondered if he was nervous, too. Then he thought of his father. *Dad would be really proud if I could bring home a goose.*

He bit his lip and closed his left eye in order to aim better.

Gently, but urgently, Grampa whispered: "Go ahead, Will. *Now!*"

In one swift motion, Will popped the safety and squeezed the trigger. An explosion tore through the air echoing harshly in the woods across the hollow. The recoil from the gun hit Will so hard it felt like someone had punched him in the shoulder and sent him reeling backward to the ground.

Stunned, but still holding the gun, Will pushed himself up only to see the whole flock scatter, unharmed.

Then he saw Grampa grabbing his chest and dropping to his knees.

"Grampa!" Will wailed. "Did I shoot you, Grampa? Did I?"

Grampa shook his head. "No," he choked out. "My heart, Will."

Will rushed to his grandfather's side and helped him to lie down on the grass. "Don't worry, Grampa. You'll be all right," he promised. The words came in a breathless rush. "I'll get help!"

He paused only once in the race home, to yank off the heavy boots that were slowing him down, and ran on in his stocking feet.

At the house, his mother was scrambling eggs. His father sat at the kitchen table talking to a stranger.

"It's Grampa!" Will burst out. "His heart! Up by the pond!"

Will's father and the stranger were out the door, his mother at the telephone, all in the same moment.

The girls started crying and Will raced back out the door after his father, stumbling and only then realizing how much his feet hurt.

"Will, wait!" his mother cried from the kitchen door. "You need to show the ambulance where to go!"

He nodded and, still trying to catch his breath, limped over to the barnyard gate where he took down the bars. He was frustrated, being forced to wait, not knowing how Grampa was doing. It seemed to take forever. But at last the flashing yellow lights appeared. A door swung open. Will climbed in and pointed directions across the pasture.

The ambulance had to go slowly because the ground was so soft from the rain. At the top of the hill overlooking the pond, it stopped. Two paramedics grabbed their equipment and followed Will down the path.

Grampa lay in the same place. Will's father kneeled beside him, holding his hand and stroking his forehead. "It'll be all right, Pop," he was saying. "They're here."

Forced to stay back, Will and his father watched as the paramedics gave Grampa oxygen and put a needle in his arm.

"He's still alive," his father said. But Will heard his voice quaver. And he wondered: Why were Grampa's eyes closed? Why wasn't he answering them?

He looked from Grampa's face, half-covered with an oxygen mask, to his father, who suddenly turned to him. The deep lines in his forehead drew together. "What the devil were you two doing up here?" he demanded.

Stunned, Will opened his mouth to explain, but there wasn't time because his father had turned to help carry the stretcher uphill.

Will followed. "Dad?" he said.

But as soon as his grandfather was loaded into the ambulance, Will's father hopped in, too, and the doors were slammed shut. The other man, who had come with his father, took the seat up front with the paramedics. Lights began flashing again and the ambulance took off without anyone asking Will if he wanted to go. Left behind, he stood frozen until the last blink of yellow disappeared.

Honk-a-ronk! Gray Feather calls out. He is alone and the sound is plaintive, issued to a silent world.

Hailstones have left a deep, bloody gash on his head. Lying at the bottom of a vine-covered ravine, he has to struggle to right himself.

He calls again, but there is no answer, only the sound of wind blowing through the tangled brush at the top of the ravine. Slowly, he climbs. But his feet catch in the vines and several times he falls.

When he reaches the top, an empty stretch of field and forest await. Everything is wet; even the air smells of damp sunshine. In the distance, a thin, silver line of water glitters in the bright daylight as if, overnight, a falling star has shattered along its surface, smashing into a thousand shining pieces. Gray Feather tries his wings, then awkwardly, delicately, folds them in and walks toward the water.

The sun is high in the sky when he arrives at the creek. All around him are signs of geese. Tufts of down are pressed into the mud by the recent rain and broken pieces of feathers are caught in the prickly stems of a nearby hedgerow.

Gray Feather drinks and preens. He tucks in one leg to nap. Still no geese come. The sun moves and shadows from the edge of the woods begin to throw themselves toward the field. Two crows bicker overhead and down at the water, a deer high-steps through the mud, its feet making loud sucking noises.

Gray Feather looks to the sky. He tries his wings again. When the wind shifts, carrying the faint sound of a barking dog, he is off.

The Killing Part

The sun beat steadily in a certain spot on Will's back making it damp and prickly. Still he didn't move. Hours passed before he even looked for his boots. When he found them, he put them on and returned to sit again by the edge of the pond, thinking, waiting.

In the distance, a dog barked and a boat horn sounded from somewhere on the Susquehanna. The shotgun lay nearby on the ground.

Will hadn't touched the gun again, but tears welled in his eyes everytime he glared at it. The gunshot, he figured, must have jolted Grampa so hard it affected his heart. It was probably the loudest noise Will had ever heard. Grampa hadn't been hunting in years. It must have been too much for him.

"Why didn't I see it?" Will asked himself out loud. "All morning, Grampa was out of breath. When we walked up the hill. When we hauled down the boat. His hands were shaking. Everything wore him out."

"I should have noticed," he told the tree nearby.

"I should have seen it!" he screamed at the sky.

He dropped his head. "Now, if I lose Grampa, I lose the only *real* friend I have. And it's my own fault. All because of a stupid hunting trip."

Kicking at the ground with his heel, he felt the anger boil up again. "I *hate* guns! I *hate* geese!"

He held his face in his hands and cried.

And now, he concluded, he hated himself, too.

He knew he wasn't supposed to hate so much. But what else could he do? Pray? He wondered about that. If he prayed really, really hard, would God forgive him for pulling the trigger and making his grandfather have a heart attack?

He doubted it. But it was worth a try. Clamping his hands together he pressed them against his forehead. *You know I didn't mean it, God. My Grampa is good. He's a good person. We need him, God. Please let Grampa live. Please, dear God. Please let Grampa live.*

Cautiously, Will looked up toward heaven, searching for some sort of sign that he'd been heard. His eyes were blurry with tears. He had to blink several times. But there was no question about it. In the sky, there was a Canada goose.

It was a solitary goose and for the briefest moment, Will found that odd. He scanned the sky, looking for others, but there weren't any.

Quickly, Will unfolded his hands, wiped at his eyes and reached for the gun.

"You little bugger," he swore angrily. "If it weren't for you stupid darn birds my Grampa would be here right now."

As if eager for the company, the goose came steadily toward the decoys.

Will stood, lifted the gun and settled it against his shoulder. The way he felt, he could have blasted a whole flock out of the sky. Fixing a bead on the bird, he took aim and fired.

Once again, a shotgun blast shattered the still air. This time, Will kept the stock pressed tightly against his cheek and the recoil jolted him, but didn't throw him to the ground.

Lowering the gun, he was startled to see the goose drop from the sky. It landed heavily, with a splash, in the shallow water near shore.

Will's mouth opened in astonishment.

He took a step forward, not really knowing why and stared in disbelief at what he had done.

Suddenly, he felt as though he was going to throw up. He steadied himself by sitting on the log. When the wave of nausea passed, he had a slipping down sensation as though everything inside had drained out of him. Even his hands and feet felt numb and weightless.

He had shot a goose. A beautiful Canada goose. He wasn't angry anymore. Nor proud. He was simply empty.

He wondered, now that he had killed something, what he was supposed to do.

Carefully, he set the gun down and walked to the water's edge. He would at least have to pull the goose out of the water. You don't just kill something and turn your back on it, he thought. No life was that meaningless.

About five feet from shore, the goose floated awkwardly on its side, one wing bent upward. Will stared at it, dreading what he had to do.

It was a long reach, but finally, he was able to grab hold of one bloody leg and pull the bird to shore. When he let go, the leg jerked back. Surprised, Will jumped to his feet, only then realizing that the goose was still alive.

The goose stirred and tried to stand, but its right leg was broken and studded with pellet wounds. As the bird crumpled, it made a pitiful, high-pitched noise.

Will covered his mouth and shuddered. He knew from his father's stories that Uncle Lester would have picked up the wounded bird and, with one quick twist of his hand, broken its neck. It had always seemed like such a horrible thing; now, Will understood how merciful it was.

Turning, he went back to the bushes and picked up the gun. There was only one way he knew to end the bird's misery. The goose was no more than ten feet away. Surely, Will told himself, he wouldn't miss from here.

Carefully, Will pressed the little button that allowed him to "break open" the gun. Then he fished inside the knapsack, found the shotgun shells and took two more. One at a time, he slid them into the empty barrels. The gun closed with a heavy click and Will stood.

He hoisted the shotgun to his shoulder and tried to take aim. But this time, the gun felt like a cannon: cold and ponderously heavy. Worse, it felt terribly wrong.

Slowly, Will knelt and set the gun down. He pushed the safety back on.

Maybe the leg will heal, he was thinking. Maybe the goose could get better and fly away—like nothing ever happened! He couldn't remember the word, but Will was thinking about reparation as he grabbed the knapsack and rushed to the water's edge.

The goose lay motionless on the grass. It was so close to death that it allowed Will to stroke its long black neck and touch its quivering, open bill.

"Don't be scared," Will said gently.

Fumbling inside his pack, Will found the First-Aid kit and flipped open the lid. The liquid iodine caught his eye. He dumped the entire bottle over the goose's injured leg, then ripped open a roll of gauze and began the wrap the leg together, where it was broken. With his teeth, he tore off a piece of white adhesive tape and made the bandage snug.

The wing was a different matter. Clearly, it, too, was broken, possibly in more than one place. Will could even see where two pellets had lodged in the bone. Wincing, he dabbed at the blood with a sterile pad and tried to apply some ointment.

The goose lay still, its brown eyes open, wide and wild. A soft breeze ruffled the black feathers on one side of its head.

"I don't know what more I can do," Will whispered. "I'm awful sorry."

He spread his jacket beside the goose and, carefully, so as not to hurt the bird even more, lifted the warm, nearly lifeless body onto the garment.

After swaddling it as best he could, Will reached underneath and delicately picked up the bundle. He cradled the injured bird in his arms, the way he used to hold Molly and Megan when they were tiny babies. Then he carried the goose, slowly, gently, all the way back to the barn.

9
Remorse

Inside the barn, the hayloft was stacked with black shadows. A bat fluttered overhead and Will hesitated. He knew the electricity had been turned off years ago. The only light in the building this late in the day came from three large windows over the sawdust bin. Will made his way there and settled the injured bird on a bed of soft wood chips.

The goose had closed its eyes, but Will could see the slight rise and fall of its chest and knew it was still alive. For a long time, he simply watched it breathe, all the while thinking of his grandfather and fearing the worst.

A car door slammed out in the yard and Will heard voices he didn't recognize. He stroked the goose one last time. "I'll be back," he promised.

Apprehensively, Will approached the house. Inside his boots, his socks were muddy and wet. His feet were sore and every step hurt. On the porch outside the kitchen he stood, hesitating. No telling how long he would have waited if Mrs. Beardsley hadn't opened the door.

Mrs. Beardsley was one of Grampa's neighbors. She was a large woman with a round red face and short, curly hair. She talked a mile a minute and had a yappy little dog named Felix that Will disliked because it nipped at his ankles.

"Well!" Mrs. Beardsley exclaimed upon seeing Will.

"Thank goodness!" Will's mother cried. "I was just about to go looking for you! I thought you went to the hospital with the ambulance—but then Dad just called and said you weren't with him!"

Will hugged his mother. It never occurred to him that anyone might be worried about *him*.

"How's Grampa?" he asked.

"He had a heart attack, Will. But he's still alive." She hugged him again and Will tried hard to hold back the tears. He didn't want to cry in front of Mrs. Beardsley, who was approaching with a sandwich on a plate.

"Alma, you'd better hold on to that for a minute," Will's mother said. "I've got to clean him up first."

"I should say," Mrs. Beardsley agreed, spying the muddy boots. "The boy looks as though he's been running through a swamp all afternoon. He'll catch his death of cold that way, you know."

It was good to get upstairs in the bathroom, away from Mrs. Beardsley and the other neighbors in Grampa's kitchen.

"When's Grampa coming home?" Will asked.

"Too early to say."

"Is he going to be all right?"

His mother shrugged and closed the lid on the toilet so Will could sit down. "We just don't know yet, Will."

Will sat down and took off his boots. "Why are all these people here?"

"It's only a few neighbors, Will. Word gets around pretty fast. They just want to help."

Gingerly, Will peeled off his socks. His mother rinsed out a clean facecloth with warm water, and began to gently wash off his feet.

"Why'd you run in your socks, Will?"

"My boots were slowing me down. I couldn't wait!"

"I want you to know how proud I am," she said. "Running all the way home like that."

"I just wish I could've done something more," Will said, biting his lower lip as his mother worked on a cut. "At first I thought I shot Grampa, you know."

She stopped and looked up at him. "You did? But why, Will? What were you doing up there with a shotgun?"

"Grampa took me hunting. It was for Dad," he told her. "Grampa said if I got a goose, Dad would let me go with him to Uncle Lester's."

"Oh, I see."

"It was Grampa's idea, Mom. Neither one of us really wanted to shoot the goose—er, shoot any goose! But we both wanted me to go hunting with Dad."

His mother waited for him to finish.

"Grampa said you can't ever tell Dad anything. You have to show him."

Will's mother smiled her understanding and began dabbing ointment on the cuts. "Well, I think we need to tell your father the whole story when he gets home."

She taped a gauze pad to one foot and put two bandages on the other.

"That should help," she said, patting his knee. But as she stood, her expression changed abruptly. "Will, your hands. Why are they so bloody? And your shirt?"

Up until now, he hadn't even noticed how much blood from the goose had spattered on him. He wondered if he should tell her. She liked animals. She rode horses when she was a girl and had a pet raccoon named Bandit. She always said it was such a shame that some raccoons got rabies because now no one wanted one for a pet. Surely, she'd understand about the goose.

But something stopped him. Embarrassment? Shame for what he had done? Grampa would be disappointed his aim fell short. And his father? Ha! His father would find it really pathetic. Will could just hear him: *The kid didn't even have the guts to kill the darn goose! How can you expect me to take him on a hunting trip?*

"Will?"

Not that Will cared anymore about the hunting trip.

"Will! What is going on? Where is this blood from?"

"I don't know, Mom. My feet?"

"Your feet?" She looked at him hard, her hands on her hips, and was about to say something more when Mrs. Beardsley tapped at the bathroom door and stuck her head inside.

"Excuse me, Miriam, there's a phone call for you."

"Probably Dad," she said to Will.

Together, they hurried into Grampa's bedroom to pick up the extension. Will stood at the foot of his grandfather's bed, listening to his mother's end of the conversation and hoping she wouldn't ask him to leave.

"Josh? Is he any better?...Oh, that's good." She sighed with relief. "So he'll stay in intensive care overnight?...Well, all we can do is wait now. Why don't you come on home? The neighbors brought some food."

Will sat quietly on the bed.

"What? Oh, really, Josh. I don't think you should take that job. What if your father takes a turn for the worse? Besides, I think you need to come home and talk to Will....Yes, I know it's an opportunity...Of course we need the money. But this isn't the time. Please, Josh."

She hung up the telephone and let her hands drop in her lap. "Your father had a job offer this morning."

"He did?"

"Do you remember the man sitting at the table? The one who ran up back with Dad?"

Will remembered.

"That was Bob Wilson," she said. "He wants your father to help him drive a moving van to San Diego."

"San Diego? You mean, in California?"

Will's mother nodded. "The trouble is, Bob needs somebody pretty quick."

She tried to smile. "The good news is that Grampa's awake."

Will rushed to throw his arms around his mother's neck.

By the time the neighbors left and the twins were in bed, Will still hadn't said anything about the goose. He tried eating one of Mrs. Beardsley's sandwiches, but couldn't, and sat in his pajamas on the living room sofa waiting for his mother to finish on the telephone.

"That was Dad again," she said. "He's going to stay at the hospital until he's sure Grampa is okay. He doesn't know what to do about this job offer."

She slumped down on the couch beside him. "Everything all at once," she said.

Will felt helpless beside her, but he wanted to say something to comfort her, to let her know he could be counted on. "It'll be all right," he tried. His mother squeezed his hand and Will decided he couldn't tell her about the goose. Not then.

It was sometime later, much later, when Will heard the back door close and realized he must have fallen asleep on the couch and been covered by the heavy red afghan Grampa kept folded on the hassock beside his favorite chair. Then he remembered the goose and began to worry, knowing it must be thirsty by now, and scared all alone in the barn.

His mother was locking the back door as he stumbled into the kitchen, still tying the sash on his bathrobe.

"Will, it's midnight. What are you doing up?"

He had a flashlight in one hand. "I need to show you something, Mom."

"What is it?"

"I have to show you. It's out in the barn."

One of the twins cried out from her crib upstairs and Will's mother looked over his head. When the cry wasn't repeated, she turned back to him. There was a pause and she said, "All right. Let's go."

The flashlight didn't provide much light, but with his mother and three cats behind him, Will wasn't afraid of entering the dark barn. When they got to the sawdust bin, he shined the light on the goose, which was still nestled in his jacket. He was relieved to see it stir and blink its eyes. Intrigued, the cats sniffed and began inching closer.

"Scat!" Will ordered, crouching protectively beside the bird. Gently, he peeled back portions of his jacket so his mother could see the goose better. She knelt quietly beside him. Her long, loose hair spilled over her shoulders and covered her face so Will couldn't see her expression. He turned back to the goose and wondered what she was thinking.

Before long, he felt her hand on his shoulder. "I think I'm beginning to understand."

The back of Will's throat began to ache. "It's going to die," Will blurted out. "Just like Grampa! And it'll be all my fault!"

"Oh, Will, come on." His mother put an arm around his shoulders and squeezed them. "Don't assume the worst. Grampa's tough. You know that. People recover from heart attacks all the time. And it's not your fault. Grampa's had heart trouble before."

Will looked up at her. "He has?"

She nodded. "That's why he sold the cows and gave up milking when he did." She tightened her embrace. "He didn't like to talk about it. And I'm not sure he was very good about taking his medicine. But you couldn't ask him about that either. Guess that's where your father gets it, huh?

"But the goose, Will. I don't know; it's been shot all over. It doesn't look very good."

Will stared at the crippled bird thinking that if it died, everything else would fall down too, like dominoes, one bad thing toppling into another. But the next thing he knew his mother was reaching beneath the bird, scooping it up.

"You've got the flashlight, Will. Take us back to the house," she said.

"No! You can't!" Will said.

"We've got to keep it warm, Will."

"But I don't want Dad to know. Please, Mom. I can't let Dad know!"

She stopped and gently pulled her hands out from under the goose. "I can't make anymore decisions today, Will. Whatever you want. But let's get him fixed up a little better. We'll make a bed in a box—to keep out the draft—and fill it with some soft rags."

Will smiled with relief.

"And let's get him some water right away. We might need an eyedropper for that."

Will was on his feet, ready to go.

"Oh—first of all, Will, gather the cats. We'll lock them on the porch tonight, to keep them away."

"Yes, Ma'am!" Will replied.

Next morning, while Will's father slept in, his mother called a local veterinarian. Will listened on the extension upstairs.

"I'm leaving for the airport, Mrs. Newcomb. I really can't take the time to look at the bird this morning," Dr. Norton said. "But I can give you the name of someone in Harrisburg."

Will cringed. He knew his mother would never take the goose all the way to Harrisburg. It was at least a half-hour drive, which meant an hour in the car altogether, a major undertaking with the twins. Besides, it was sure to be expensive.

"Can you at least advise us on what to do?"

"Well, the important thing is that the wound is clean and antiseptic has been applied. Once you get the goose to someone, they'll tape the broken wing into a flex position—you know, a normal, closed-wing position."

"Ah. Un-huh. Okay."

Will could tell that his mother was taking notes.

"The only other thing I'd say, Mrs. Newcomb, is that if the bird was shot with lead pellets, it might simply die from lead poisoning despite all your efforts."

"Lead poisoning?"

"Lead is toxic. If it gets into the system the bird may die. Lead shot is not legal, you understand. Law requires hunters to use steel shot now," Dr. Norton explained. "But there are a lot of old-timers who still have the lead shot around. I'm just telling you this so you don't get your hopes up."

"So if the shot was lead, the bird will die." His mother made it sound so matter of fact.

"Antibiotics might save it. Maybe. To be honest, lead poisoning is far more common in geese who have picked up spent pellets while grazing in a cornfield as opposed to those who have been shot."

"I see. Well, I certainly thank you, Dr. Norton."

Will and his mother gathered up some supplies and returned to the barn. They gave the goose more water, one drop at a time, with the eyedropper. Then they painstakingly picked out every pellet they could find with a sterilized sewing needle and tweezers.

The hardest part was fashioning a crude splint out of popsicle sticks and adhesive tape for the broken wing.

"One more time," Will's mother said as she positioned the stick and Will held the wing. On their fourth effort, they finally succeeded.

The twins watched and were surprisingly good about staying out of the way.

"Goose sick," Molly kept saying. "Mommy, goose sick."

"Yes, yes. The goose is very sick," Will's mother replied.

Megan kept pushing a piece of her English muffin toward the goose, but the bird lay motionless, its eyes closed. Will stroked it on the neck with one finger.

"How would we know if they were lead pellets?" he asked.

"I'm not sure, Will. Was there a box or something?"

Vaguely, Will remembered the box with the shotgun shells. That reminded him that the gun and all the decoys, even the knapsack, were still back at the pond.

After lunch, Will returned to fetch everything, including the shotgun shells. The box rattled as he lifted it to read the label: Remington Number 2, Lead Pellets.

He was tempted, then, to heave the box into the pond. But he remembered the veterinarian's words about the geese getting sick from eating the pellets in the field. If fish ate them, they might get sick, too. Will felt good about remembering this in time and dropped the shot shells into his pocket.

Back at home, in the kitchen, the first thing Will saw when he walked in was his jacket, hung out to dry on a rack near the wood stove. He lifted the end of one damp sleeve and was relieved to see that his mother was able to wash all the blood out. There was no doubt in his mind now. Will pulled the shot shells out of his pocket and put them where he figured they belonged: in the trash basket.

10

Point of View

The worries went round and round in Will's mind. Would his grandfather live? Was his father going to drive a moving van all the way to San Diego? Was the goose going to live? What did geese eat anyway?

On the bus Monday morning Will found it hard to concentrate on any one thing and so he sat staring out the window, letting all the scenery—the fields and farms and houses—blur together.

He had hoped he could stay home, but Molly didn't feel well and Will's mother said she had her hands full.

I pledge allegiance to the flag of the United State of America...

During the pledge, Will found himself mouthing the familiar words and wondering if someone would think to get Grampa a pipe at the hospital. Even if he couldn't smoke it, it would probably make him feel more at home if he had his pipe. Then maybe he'd recuperate faster.

One nation, under God...

Under God? Indeed! Will thought to himself. Where was God when you needed him?

After the pledge Ms. Ritter picked up a pot of yellow chrysanthemums. "Just one minute before we start," she said, going to the sink at the back of the room. "I forgot to water my flowers."

Hearing the water run made Will worry that his mother would forget to give the goose a drink.

A boy named Gary Winslow had a black rubber bat, the Halloween kind, and was bouncing it up and down on a long piece of elastic, like a yo-yo. Everyone else in class was giggling and whispering. Everyone except him, that is.

Ms. Ritter set the flowers back down on her desk and began handing out white, lined paper. Gary hung the bat on the back of his chair.

Suddenly, Will felt the blood rush to his face. They would be writing book reports in class and he had forgotten to read even a single page of his book!

"I want everything except a pen in your desk or under your chair," Ms. Ritter ordered.

In his mind he could see the book sitting on the bureau in his room back at Grampa's. *The Island of the Blue Dolphins* by Scott O'Dell. Ms. Ritter had given it to him Friday when he told her what a good reader he was. It had 184 pages and was about a girl with long black hair who lived alone on an island in the sea. But that was all Will knew about the book. And it was definitely not enough to fake a book report.

"We're going to do something different today," Ms. Ritter announced cheerily, making Will's pain all the sharper. "I want you to identify an emotion you felt while reading your book and then apply it to someone else."

She ignored all the puzzled looks she was getting and kept handing out paper.

"It's really quite simple," she continued. "If your story was about a dangerous mountain climbing expedition, then maybe you felt afraid while reading it. Fear is the emotion. Maybe you describe the fear your little brother endured the first time he went to the dentist.

"Remember we talked about point of view on Friday?" She headed back toward her desk. "Put yourself in someone else's shoes."

Will stared at the blank paper on his desk and thought about the cover of his book again: a young girl, spear in hand, poised on the edge of a cliff. She was looking out to sea, wasn't she? Probably waiting for someone to come and rescue her. Gosh. If only he'd read the first chapter. If only he'd read the blurb on the back cover!

"This is a book report?" Gary Winslow complained as he slumped over his desk.

"Actually, it's more of a creative writing assignment," Ms. Ritter replied crisply. "Have fun with it!"

Gary moaned and slid down into his seat.

Nervous, Will sat up stiffly. As he did, something pinched him in his pants pocket. He reached in and felt the Optic Wonder. He took it with him everywhere. Now, as he traced the smooth lens with his thumb, he thought of the last time he used the Optic Wonder. It was Saturday, when he and Grampa were searching the sky for geese.

Will pulled the Optic Wonder from his pocket and looked at it sadly. A lone goose in the sky. A lone girl on an island. Even though he'd never been stranded on an island, Will knew what it was like to be lonely. He thought about how, at night, at the farm, he would lie with his head at the bottom of his bed so he could look out the window and watch for his father's truck. And almost every night, as he lay there watching for the two headlights that meant his father was home, he would fall asleep and wake up cold because he was at the wrong end of the bed without any covers.

"Emotion," Ms. Ritter emphasized one more time by writing the word on the blackboard. "Did your book make you laugh? Did it make you sad?"

A girl alone. A goose alone. Will's mind was busy as thoughts crisscrossed and jumped back and forth like electricity.

"Point of view," Miss Ritter added, underlining the phrase with several brisk strokes of white chalk. When she finished, she clapped the chalk dust from her hands and the room became silent.

Was it possible? Will wondered to himself. Could he pull this off? He set the Optic Wonder down in front of him for inspiration, found his pen and began to write. The more he wrote, the faster he went.

When the papers began arriving on her desk, Ms. Ritter put on her glasses and started to read.

"I can see that some of you had a good time with this," she said. "I also see that it's time for recess."

As the rest of the class lined up at the door to go outside, Will lingered at his desk. He still hadn't turned in the assignment. Now, he wondered if he dared.

Ms. Ritter was gathering the sheets into a neat pile in the middle of her desk.

Quickly, Will delivered his paper and fled the room.

He figured it would be several days before he heard anything about the writing assignment. It never occurred to him that Ms. Ritter would use her lunch hour later that day to look through the papers. Or that she'd read some of them aloud that very afternoon!

Suddenly, Will felt queasy.

Sarah Lacey's assignment was right on target, Ms. Ritter said before she began reading it. It was about a girl their age who worried about being cast aside upon the birth of a new baby brother. Gee whiz, Will thought, she ought to be glad her mother didn't have twins!

"Looks like we only have time for one more," Ms. Ritter said lifting the next paper from the top of the pile.

She began to read aloud: "My book was *The Island of the Blue Dolphins*, by Scott O'Dell."

Every muscle in his body froze. Unbelievable, Will thought to himself. Of all the kids in class…

"In this book, the main character has long hair and lives alone on an island. She is afraid sometimes. But mostly she's lonely. She stands on a cliff and watches the sea. She hopes she'll spot a white sail or a puff of smoke…"

Deep in his pocket, Will clenched the Optic Wonder so hard one of the lenses popped out.

11

The Goose Project

"Will, would you like to read this yourself?" Ms. Ritter stopped to ask.

Weakly, Will shook his head.

"All right then, I'll continue." She cleared her throat, adjusted her eyeglasses and began reading:

"The emotion is loneliness.

"I am a Canada goose. Somehow, I got separated from the others in my flock. I am alone. It's scary. But mostly it's lonely. When I honk, no one answers. When I fly, there is no one to cut a path for me. I keep on flying anyway because if I stop I think I might die from loneliness.

"One day while I'm flying I see a little pond with a flock of geese on it! Man, am I excited! My feet go out for a landing. Only halfway down this weird feeling sinks in. These geese are not moving. They're not even turning to look at me. They're stiff as wood.

"Suddenly, there is a loud noise and it feels like dynamite has exploded in my body. I fall from the sky into the pond. The water is cold and black. Pure liquid loneliness, I think.

"Before I pass out, two thoughts go through my mind. First, I think, what a dirty trick. Second, I think about my father who is flying on without me. One day, I tell myself, I'll catch up. I will again fly with my father, who promised me that one day I would lead the flock all the way to Maryland. When I think of that, there is hope deep in my heart. When I think of that, I am a little less lonely."

When Ms. Ritter finished reading, everyone turned to look at Will.

"Some exellent writing," his teacher said.

At first, Will was embarrassed. If he could have, he would have slid right under his desk and pulled his sweater over his head.

"Very creative," Ms. Ritter added.

It wasn't though and Will knew it. The goose was real. It had bloody feathers and a broken leg and a wing that might never work again. It had a black bill that lay awkwardly open and moist dark eyes that once glistened and blinked and watched for trouble.

Will felt himself gripping the edge of his desk.

"I want you all to regard Will's essay as a good example of how you can free up your mind," Ms Ritter was saying.

"Excuse me, Ms. Ritter," Will said suddenly. He stood, softly scraping back his chair. "But it wasn't very creative. Not at all, in fact."

One by one, every head in class turned around until twenty pairs of eyes were riveted on him.

Will took a breath. "It's just the truth is all. I didn't free up my mind like you said, Ms. Ritter, and make it up. The Canada goose is at my Grampa's—in a box in the barn. But I'm not sure it's going to live. My Mom and I gave it water. We picked out the pellets with a needle, but we're not sure we got them all.

"Then we taped up the wing. It took us a long time. It's hard, getting the tape to stick to the feathers and all."

He paused. "Now I don't know what else to do."

Looking out into the faces in class, Will opened his hands and half-shrugged. "I don't know what geese eat," he said. "I don't know what they need!"

The room was stone quiet. Even Ms. Ritter was speechless. She took off her glasses and moistened her lips. Will's eyes skimmed over the class once more and quickly, he sat down.

"Will, this is extraordinary," Ms. Ritter began thoughtfully. "You have an injured goose. A bird that some hunter shot and left to die?"

He hesitated, suddenly realizing he hadn't exactly told the whole truth about the situation. But he nodded anyway. At least he hadn't lied.

"How could somebody be that cruel?" Ms. Ritter asked.

Evelyn Potter's hand went up, but she didn't wait to be called on. "My uncle had some Canada geese that used to live at his farm," she said. "They ate some kind of grass. He planted it for them. I'll call him tonight and see if I can go over and get some for Will's goose."

"Corn!" Larry Praeger called out, turning to Will at the same time. "I know they like corn. All geese like corn!"

"I have some popcorn I can bring!" another offered.

"Popcorn?! If we have popcorn, can we watch a movie, Ms. Ritter?" It was Gary Winslow, who was twirling the rubber bat over his head.

"We could build it a house!" someone called out.

"Will could bring it to school one day!"

"I think he ought to just wring its neck!" someone else called out, startling Will.

Ms. Ritter came down the aisle to take the bat from Gary and held up her hand to get everyone's attention.

"People! People!"

She waited for it to quiet down. "Why don't we all do a little research tonight and find out what Canada geese eat? Then, maybe, we can help Will."

She smiled at him and Will felt better. But deep inside, the truth of what he had done lay heavy, dragging down every good feeling that surfaced. Sure, he may look like a hero to the class, but Will had failed to tell them he pulled the trigger himself and shot the goose with poisonous lead pellets. Should he tell them now? No, he thought, because if the police found out, they might arrest him! And then Grampa would get in trouble, too, because Will wasn't twelve years old!

Will decided to just hold the whole truth in reserve until he could get home and sort things out. It wasn't his fault that strange things started happening that day at school. Like at the end of school, when Larry Praeger and Tommy Leipsic both walked with him to his locker. Tommy even offered him a chocolate-covered granola bar, and didn't ask for anything in trade. He said it was "awesome" about the goose.

Then, just before he got on the bus, Sarah Lacey tapped Will on the arm. "It was very nice of you to save the Canada goose," she said. "I love animals, too. I have a brown-and-white guinea pig named Ebenezer."

"Neat," Will said, turning quickly to hop up the steps.

12
The Promise

When the school bus pulled away, Will was already racing up Grampa's long driveway. After bounding up the back steps two at a time, he arrived, breathless, in the kitchen, where his mother was putting groceries away. Megan was stomping down the paper bags and Molly lay on the kitchen floor whimpering.

"How's Grampa?" Will asked. "How's my goose?"

His words were drowned out by Molly's screams.

"Another ear infection!" Will's mother said loudly. "We had to go to the doctor!"

"Did you give the goose a drink?" Will shouted.

She shook her head. "I'm sorry, Will—"

Molly kicked her feet and got Will right in the ankle. "Ow!" he exclaimed.

"I didn't have time!" Will's mother said, throwing up her hands. "Today's been awful!"

"What about Grampa?" Will demanded.

His mother was bent over, trying to scoop up Molly. "No change."

Disgusted, Will grabbed the eyedropper from the kitchen counter, filled a cup with water and walked quickly to the barn.

He sat, cross-legged, his jacket still on, beside his injured bird. "Come on," he urged, trying to coax the goose into opening its bill so he could get in a drop of water.

Megan wandered into the sawdust bin a few minutes later, holding her stuffed rabbit. She stood quietly beside Will.

At school, there had been a glimmer of hope. But now, Will didn't think the goose could possibly live. He would never bring it to school. And he would have to live with what he had done. He was sorry he had ever told the kids at school about the goose.

When his mother knelt beside him, Will didn't even look up.

"I'm sorry I forgot about the goose," she said gently. "I hope you'll forgive me. There was so much happening today. On top of everything else, your father decided to help drive that moving van. He says we need the money."

"But what about Grampa? Isn't Dad worried?" Will asked.

"Sure he's worried," his mother said. 'But Grampa's in the hospital where he's getting help and his condition has stabilized. There's nothing more any of us can do except pray and wait to see how he recovers."

Will saw that his mother had a small bottle of pink liquid in her hands.

"Look," she said. "Why don't we give the goose some of Molly's amoxicillin? It's an antibiotic. I'll call the doctor and tell him I spilled the first prescription. We'll use the refill for the goose."

Will stared at her. "You can do that?"

His mother smiled sheepishly. "Well, I won't tell if *you* don't."

This was the best idea Will had heard all day.

Gently, with two hands, he pried open the bird's bill so his mother could get in a dropper full of medicine.

"I'd better stay," he told his mother, "in case he wakes up and needs me."

"Good idea," she agreed. "I'll call you for dinner."

For a long time, Will and Megan watched the goose, but it remained still with its eyes closed.

Finally, Will took Megan back to the house and got his math homework, which he worked on in the sawdust bin. He figured he might as well get something done while waiting for the goose to wake up. Long division was not Will's favorite. It seemed as though his remainders were always bigger than his divisors and that he had to start the problem all over again.

A few minutes later, Megan reappeared, this time with her rabbit, a naked doll and a soft purple dinosaur wearing a green jacket back-ward. She propped them up at the end of the box facing the goose.

Will watched her, amused, and noticed for the first time that Megan's beloved rabbit had only one eye now and that the doll was missing a chunk of hair on the back of its head. What a bunch of misfits, he thought. Not just the stuffed animals and the doll, either—but Megan who didn't talk, and the goose who couldn't fly, and even Will, himself, who didn't know where he fit in anymore.

"Thanks, Megs," he said, leaning over to pat her on the head. "Now if the goose wakes up when we're not here, he won't be lonely."

Pleased, Megan nodded shyly. Then, with the tip of one pudgy finger, she stroked the goose on its neck, just as Will had been doing.

Long after he had finished his homework and Megan had returned to the house, Will heard footsteps coming through the barn. Probably his mother, he thought, coming to get him for dinner. But when he looked up he saw his father.

His father sat beside him, but Will said nothing, just kept staring at the goose which remained motionless, its bill open enough to expose a narrow, pointed tongue. Will felt such sympathy for the animal that he didn't care anymore if his father had discovered the truth.

"Mom told me all about it," his father said. "And I want you to know I'm not mad. I'm certainly not ashamed, Will. Far from it. Because now I know why you and Grampa were up there."

Will said nothing.

"I understand what happened, Will. And I don't think you're a coward. In fact, I think you're pretty brave. It would have been a whole lot easier to leave it to die by the pond. Or pull the trigger again and be done with it."

His father sighed. "You obviously listened to something deeper inside. You've got a good heart, son. I'm proud of you for it. That's nothing to ever be ashamed of."

Will looked at his Dad, surprised to hear this coming from him.

There was a pause. His father looked at him. "But I still don't think you should have been out there shooting, Will. The law is there for a reason. So kids like you know all the safety rules and how to handle a gun before you go out and start shootin' it off."

"But Grampa showed me!"

"I know, I know. Still, you got to do what the law says, Will."

All along that part had bothered him. "I'm sorry, Dad," he said. "I really am."

"I know you are." His father's eyes met his. "And I want you to know I'm sorry, too. Sorry for the way I've been. I don't suppose you can understand." He tried to smile, but couldn't quite. "I'm not sure I understand. I guess what I want to say is that I'm just sorry for not being a better father lately. I want you to know when I get back we'll fix up the Willard. I know I've said that before and didn't do anything. But this time things will be different."

Will kept looking at him, hard, because it seemed to him he had heard this before.

"I promise you, Will," his father said, "the first thing you'll see in my hand is a new spark plug."

Will smiled finally, and enjoyed the feel of his father's hand on his shoulder. Together, silently, they turned back to the goose.'

"I don't hold out much hope for it," Will said.

"No. I wouldn't, Will. It's been hurt pretty bad. But I do know one thing."

"What's that?" Will asked. "I think it'll do a lot better if it's kept warmer. Your mother suggested we move it into the kitchen. Set the box by the wood stove."

"Think we can?"

His father grinned. "I know we can."

And so the goose moved into the house, just as Will's father prepared to move out onto the road with a man named Bob Wilson who owned a moving van.

Will's mother made a nice spaghetti dinner with lots of garlic bread, which Will and his father loved. But no one seemed to have much appetite, especially Will's mother, and the meal was quiet.

Just as they were finishing, they heard a loud, heavy motor coming up the hill.

"That'll be Bob," Will's father said.

Will went to the window in the kitchen door and pushed the curtain aside. It was starting to drizzle but Will could see the huge silver tractor cab as it rolled up to the back door. There wasn't a big trailer hooked onto the back of it yet so it looked kind of funny, like a turtle without its shell.

His father kissed the twins good-bye and Will stood behind them, waiting. When it was his turn, though, his mother began to cry. Will's father reached out to her, but she pulled away.

"Things'll be fine, Miriam," he said. "I'll be back in two or three weeks, depending on what we pick up out there."

She shook her head. "No. I have a bad feeling about it. I don't want you to go. We need you here, Josh."

"I thought we talked about that," his father said.

"I just don't think you should go, Josh."

"Don't start in, Miriam. I need this job. You know that."

"But we need you, too! We need you here!"

"Get ahold of yourself, Miriam. For crying out loud." He sounded angry now. "You know how long I've tried to get work! How can you take this away from me?"

"Please!" There were tears in her eyes and both hands were clamped, up to her mouth. Will glanced at Molly and Megan and they looked scared. He took their hands and pulled them back.

"Darn it, Miriam. It's like even my own family is against me now!" He reached down by the kitchen door to grab a duffel bag, paused, and then left hurriedly, slamming the door behind him so hard the curtain rod fell off.

Will's mother ran upstairs crying.

It was a long time later, after the girls and his mother went to bed that Will put the curtain rod back up and turned on the back-porch light. Just in case.

He stood, looking out into the driving rain, not knowing what to think or how to feel. The goose, its eyes opened now, was in a box by the wood stove. Will would go and sit by him in a minute. But for now, he simply stood, watching a puddle fill up at the bottom of the stairs outside.

13

Autumn Journey

At school the next morning, Sarah Lacey handed Will a huge oil painting. In it, long straight rows of cornstalk stubble paralleled each other and ran, like railroad tracks, to the horizon. Above the field, a full moon, round and white, rose in the blue-gray evening sky, while a flock of Canada geese took flight, linking earth and sky in one frozen moment.

"I know it's only a picture," Sarah apologized. "And it's kind of scratched up because it's been in our basement next to Daddy's workbench. But if you hang it over your goose's box maybe he'll feel less lonely."

"Gee, thanks," Will said, taking the large, framed painting with both hands. It was heavy. He wondered what the bus driver would say when she saw it.

A tight group had gathered around Will and even though the bell had rung Ms. Ritter wasn't making anyone sit down.

Evelyn Potter had brought in a shiny black garbage bag full of wet grass, roots and all. Olney 3 square, she called it. She said her uncle was sure Will's goose would love it.

If that didn't perk up the bird's appetite, Will could refer to the chart Larry Praeger had made. Using colored markers Larry had listed more than a dozen different things geese ate: orchard grass, clover, Olney 3 square, wild rice, arrowhead, wild millet, smartweed, spike rush, nut grass, bulrush, wild celery, rice, corn, wheat and an occasional bug!

Of course, Will had no idea where he'd find most of these things. He'd never even heard of some of them.

Ms. Ritter clapped her hands. "Let's sit down. Then we can take turns telling Will what we learned."

Pleased, Will leaned the picture against his desk, then took his seat and sat tall.

Linda Nordstrom was first. Holding up a small bag of gravel, she glanced around the classroom to be sure she had everyone's attention. "It's grit," she announced proudly. "Every once in awhile geese need grit. It aids in their digestion. I read that in the encyclopedia. My mother laughed. She said to run out to the driveway, get some little rocks and stuff and put it in a Baggie."

Linda walked over to Will's desk and handed him the small plastic bag. Will acknowledged the gift with a simple nod.

One by one, other things were delivered: an old baby blanket for warmth, two ears of dried corn, a porcelain water bowl and a picture of the tundra from a 1989 Canadian calendar. In his squeaky, high voice, Bill Martin read what was printed underneath:

"The tundra of northern Quebec is an open plain, with scattered ponds nestled between ridges of gray rock and gravel. Vegetation is sparse: short, scrub brush and small patches of cotton grass. Each spring, hundreds of Canada geese return from the south to nest here and raise their young."

So many things had accumulated that at day's end Ms. Ritter suggested they pile everything into the back of her station wagon. "I called your mother," Ms. Ritter told Will. "She said it would be okay if I drove you home."

"Golly," he said, amazed at the prospect of riding anywhere in Ms. Ritter's car. While she locked supplies in her cabinet, Will gathered all his things and put them into an empty cardboard box his teacher had found.

He lifted the painting Sarah Lacey had given him and blew at some dust as he laid it down on his desk. It almost sent a chill up his spine, seeing the geese in flight. At the bottom of the heavy wooden frame he discovered the words *Autumn Journey* etched on a rusty metal plate. It made him wonder where his goose had been heading when he took it from the sky. And what had happened to its family.

Inside, he discovered, there was still a sore spot. He hoped it wouldn't always hurt this much, knowing he had shot the goose.

"Can I go too?"

Will looked up, surprised to see Larry Praeger standing beside his desk. All the other fifth graders had left.

"I don't think so, Larry," Ms Ritter said. "But maybe Will could invite you over one day after school. What do you think, Will?"

At first, Will hesitated and averted his eyes. He was supposed to be keeping to himself. That was the plan anyway. But Larry did make that great food chart. Will thought of all the work that must have gone into it. He looked up at the red-headed boy and wondered if Larry liked to make tree forts. "It's okay with me," Will said timidly. "If you want to."

Larry nodded eagerly. "Sure I do!" he said, and then dashed out of the classroom to catch his bus.

Ms. Ritter tucked *Autumn Journey* under one arm and Will carried the box. He kind of wished there were more kids around to see him as he accompanied his teacher down the hall and out to the parking lot where they loaded everything into the back of Ms. Ritter's station wagon.

The car was neat as a pin and had a new car smell, Will thought as he buckled himself in. Not like his mother's, which had a layer of cracker crumbs on all the seats, sticky splotches of dried juice on the dash and an assortment of plastic baby toys on the floor, front and back. The ride to his grandfather's farm would only take about ten minutes, but Will suddenly wished the trip was more like an hour.

"I'm sorry to hear about your grandfather," Ms. Ritter commented.

Will looked at her, surprised she knew.

"I can't go see him yet," he said. "He's still in intensive care and they don't let kids in."

"Hopefully, they'll move him soon," his teacher said.

Will nodded. "Hopefully. Yes."

"I get the feeling your grandfather is a pretty special person to you."

"He is," Will replied. "My grandfather is my best friend, Ms. Ritter. When he comes home, I'd like you to meet him."

"I'd be privileged," she replied.

Will knew he should have said something more, to keep up his end of the conversation. But he didn't want to risk saying something stupid that would make her laugh at him.

"You know, Will, I'm also sorry to hear your father's been out of work for so long."

Will turned to her quickly. "But he's got a job now. He's driving a moving van to San Diego."

"Yes. So your mother says. But I imagine it's been pretty hard on your family. I don't know if this is any comfort to you, Will, but a lot of families are going through the same thing. Times are tough. Companies are letting people go because they can't afford to keep them on."

Will turned to look out his window. It made him uncomfortable, talking about this.

Ms. Ritter seemed to sense how he was feeling. "It's nothing to be embarrassed about," she said. "It's not your father's fault. Good people are losing their jobs because of the economy not because of something they've done. Do you understand that, Will?"

He nodded, but continued to stare out his window. He knew that *times were not good.* It's just that knowing *why* didn't help much. It didn't change the way things were.

"In fact," Ms. Ritter went on, "if the Blackstone School Board makes any more budget cuts, I'll lose my job, too."

Will swung his head around. "You will?"

She smiled. "Don't worry. It won't happen this year. But you see, I'm new. If anyone goes, it'll be me."

"Gee," Will said, frowning. "What will you do, Ms. Ritter?"

"Oh, I don't know," she said. "I'll find something. Maybe another teaching job. I also like working with plants and flowers. Sometimes I daydream about getting a job with a florist—maybe opening my own shop. Even though I was trained to be a teacher, Will, it's not the only thing I can do. It might be different if I'd spent my whole life teaching. But goodness, I'm only twenty-three."

Will's father was much older than that. Thirty-five or thirty-six at least. And working at the port was the only job he'd ever had. Maybe, Will thought, his father didn't think he could do anything else. No. He shook his head. His father was real smart about a lot of different things. But maybe other people didn't think his father could do anything else. Maybe that was why driving the moving van was so important. To prove to everybody he could do something else.

Gosh. Will wondered if his mother had ever thought of that.

Ms. Ritter drove on, past the little shopping center with the pizza parlor, the Shear Pleasure Hair Salon, and the convenience store where Will's mother stopped for milk and diapers. From there, it was exactly one mile to his grandfather's driveway. Will pointed it out and Ms. Ritter proceeded slowly up the hill.

Will's mother and the twins were waiting on the back steps. They waved as Ms. Ritter pulled up.

"Did you know my sisters were twins?" Will asked.

"No, I didn't, Will. How exciting."

Will knew better than that. The twins were not exciting, but they were cute and fun to introduce. He popped his seat belt off and scrambled out of the car quickly.

Rushing around to Ms. Ritter's side of the car, he made hasty introductions. "This is my mother, Ms. Ritter, and my sisters, Molly and Megan."

Ms. Ritter shook hands with Will's mother and said, "Well, hi there!" to the twins. The girls backed away shyly but Ms. Ritter still made a big deal over them. "My, aren't you pretty!" Enough was enough, Will thought. The twins had a way of taking over and he was eager to get Ms. Ritter inside.

"How's my goose doing, Mom?"

"Better—much better!" she exclaimed, opening the door for them. "In fact, he's been awake most of the day and drank some water on his own."

"Really?" Will felt genuinely happy—as though someone had given him a gift.

Inside the kitchen, they gathered around the cardboard box. Ms. Ritter knelt to touch the goose on one wing. It was still lying down, but its eyes were open and it seemed alert.

"He's a young one, isn't he?" Ms. Ritter said thoughtfully. "If you're not careful, Will, the bird will want to stay around the farm the rest of its life."

Will frowned. "What do you mean?"

"This goose has had a traumatic experience and you're the one nursing it to health. It's likely to lose its fear of man and simply stay on at the farm and follow you around."

"You mean it could become a real pet?" Will asked. "Neat!"

Ms. Ritter pressed her lips together and paused before answering. "If that's what you want. I just thought that maybe you'd rather return the goose to the wild one day. To be with its own kind."

Will grew quiet, remembering. *Maybe the goose could get better and fly away, like nothing ever happened.*

"Well! It's certainly a beautiful goose, Will. You'll have to bring it to school one day soon so all the children can see it." Ms. Ritter stood and brushed off her skirt.

After she left, Will sat beside the goose. His mother had taken the girls outside to play and he was alone. *Autumn Journey* stood propped against the wooden legs of a kitchen chair nearby. Will crossed his arms and contemplated the painting. So what if he kept this goose for a pet? What difference would it make? There were a million Canada geese in the world! Anyway, he doubted the goose would ever fly again. He'd pretty much taken care of that.

"Who cares?" Will asked aloud. Then, abruptly, he stood up and carried the painting into the dining room where he leaned it, face in, against a far wall.

14
A Fire Line

Will was sitting on his bed, sorting baseball cards, when the telephone rang and his mother called upstairs to him. He hadn't had a single phone call since they moved to the farm. He hoped it was his best friend, Robbie, calling from Baltimore.

"It's Dad," came a faraway voice over the telephone line.

Astonished, Will glanced at his mother.

"Dad? Where are you?"

"Cincinnati."

"Cincinnati? Where's that?"

"Ohio, Will. Mom will show you on a map."

Will turned to his mother again. "Gee, Mom, Do we have a map?"

She was waving her hand impatiently. "We'll find one. Don't worry about that. Talk to your father, he's calling long distance."

"So. Dad. Are you almost to San Diego?"

"Not exactly," he said. "Our truck broke down. We're spending the night in a motel."

"Gosh." Will was envious. He'd never stayed in a motel before.

"Does it have a TV?" Will asked.

Will's father laughed. "Yeah, it has a TV."

"Cable?"

"I don't know. We haven't turned it on."

"Mom went to see Grampa today," Will told him. "She talked to him a little bit."

"Good!"

"But she said when she got there, he was asleep, sitting up."

"He must be tired," Will's father said.

"No, it's because if he lies down, he can't breathe good."

"Oh."

"I miss him," Will said. "I miss you."

"I miss you, too," his father said. They paused for a moment because of static on the line. "Just one more thing, Will."

"Yeah?"

"I'm sorry I didn't get to hug you good-bye."

"It's okay," Will mumbled.

"Take care of everybody," you hear?"

"I will," he answered.

His mother took the phone back and told him that Grampa was still in intensive care. "He's having some trouble breathing," she added. Will watched her, cradling the receiver in her hand, smiling at the sound of his father's voice. "I love you. I'm sorry," she said. "It's okay. Come home." All of which confused Will. He couldn't understand how two people could hate each other so much one minute and love each other the next.

After hanging up the telephone, his mother sighed, deep and heavy. Then she stood and rifled through the bookshelves over the television until she found an old road map of the United States. She unfolded it on the living room floor and kneeled down beside Will.

"Mom," Will said. "Can I ask you something?"

"Sure."

"I just don't understand," he said. "I mean, how come you're so nice to Dad on the phone and say you miss him and all that, but then when he's here, you guys fight all the time?"

"Will, I love your father," she said. "It's just that it's hard when there's no money for anything. It creates a lot of tension. And with Dad out of work there's no routine anymore. The girls are demanding. You know that. And now with Grampa in the hospital I've got to take care of all his affairs, too.

"There's all this—this *stuff* going on," she said. "And sometimes it's hard to know what's right, what's best. I try to be brave, but inside, sometimes, I'm really scared."

Will waited for her to go on.

"I guess I do snap sometimes," she said, as though realizing it for the first time. She looked at him, her eyes were soft and sad. "But I don't mean to, Will."

"I know you don't," he said.

Both of them played with the edge of the map that was spread out on the floor.

"Well. Anyway, here's Cincinnati," his mother said, pointing with her index finger.

Will put his finger next to hers in the middle of Ohio and searched for San Diego at the bottom of California. "Wow," he noted, "he has a long way to go."

"He does," his mother agreed. She pushed the hair out of his eyes.

Molly and Megan came into the room and tried to walk on the map. Will folded it and took it upstairs to his room where he spread it out again and thumbtacked it to one wall. He didn't think Grampa would mind since the wallpaper was peeling off anyway.

After popping the loose lens back in his Optic Wonder, he examined Cincinnati close up. It was right in the corner of Ohio, near Indiana and Kentucky. If you lived in Cincinnati, Will discovered, you could easily visit three states in no time!

He stuck a red thumbtack in Cincinnati, a green one on San Diego and a yellow one on Blackstone, Pennsylvania. He was thinking of adding a blue one on Baltimore when a sharp noise started him.

Dropping the tack, he whipped around.

Honk-a-ronk!

It was the goose downstairs!

It honked so loud that everyone ran to the kitchen at the same time and stopped in the doorway.

"Quiet!" Will warned them. "We don't want to scare it."

The goose was standing up in its box. It turned its head and watched them, sideways.

Slowly, carefully, Will took a step toward it.

The bird didn't move.

Will took another step.

When still the bird did not move, Will took a few more slow steps, then reached out and touched its uninjured side.

Will's mother watched and held back the girls. "Looks like you're going to have to find a name for this goose, Will. I think he's going to pull through!"

"A name," he repeated, "Gosh, Mom, what can we name him?"

Honk-a-ronk! The goose called out again, filling the house with its wild noise.

Molly jumped back and clung to her mother's leg, but Megan followed Will and stood tight against him. Unafraid, she, too, reached out her hand and touched the goose.

The goose didn't move.

And Megan said, "Gooz honk a lot."

Will's mother gasped. "Megan!"

She and Will stared at each other, astonished, not quite sure they had really heard Megan speak.

Just then, the goose honked again.

"Gooz honk a lot," Megan repeated, turning to smile at her mother.

Will's mother rushed over and wrapped her arms around Megan while Will tried to find one of her small hands to squeeze.

"Yes, he does, Megs! Good girl! He does honk a lot," Will said happily. "In fact, we'll name him Honkalot. It sort of sounds like an old Indian name, Doesn't it, Mom?"

Will's mother nodded emphatically and Will wasn't sure if she was laughing or crying. "I think it's a wonderful name!"

"Honkalot!" Will proclaimed. He reached behind his mother to pull Molly over. The four of them watched the goose while the goose watched them.

His mother was so happy tears ran down her cheeks. It made Will realize that sometimes there was a fine line between happiness and sorrow. For amidst all the joy of this moment, he couldn't help but think of Grampa, struggling to breathe in a hospital bed, and an empty shotgun, wrapped in burlap and hidden, deep in the attic, on top of a dusty wardrobe.

15

November Sun

Cincinnati, Ohio
Amarillo, Texas
Fresno, California

Will stood in his room, admiring the pattern his colored thumbtacks and red yarn had made over the last few weeks. Pretty soon he'd be able to stick a tack in Seattle, pull the yarn all the way up to Washington and then the pattern would be really neat.

After the moving van had broken down a second time and Bob Wilson said he couldn't afford to fix it, let alone pay anybody, his father had hitched a ride to Fresno, where he called late one night—he was always calling late at night after Will was in bed—to tell them he was on his way to Seattle. He knew someone there who said he could get work on a fishing boat.

"Is he always gone this long?"

It was Larry Praeger asking. The red-haired boy with the freckled face sat on Will's bed eating a Fruit Roll-Up and looking through one of Will's baseball card albums. Will had hundreds of cards, arranged by teams in several different loose-leaf binders. Every time Larry came over, he pulled one of the scrapbooks down and poured through it.

"No, he's not usually gone this long," Will said.

Larry flipped a page in the scrapbook. "Do you have a picture of him?" he asked.

"Sure." Will had a picture of his parents, their arms around each other, standing behind Will who sat in the Willard Seymour. It was the first day he drove it. Will's Uncle Lester took the picture. Will remembered because Uncle Lester practically lay on his stomach in the grass to get the right shot.

Briefly, Will looked at the images of his parents, especially his mother, whose face seemed rounder then. It had a glow to it as well, a shine that wasn't there anymore.

He handed the framed photograph to Larry and sat on the floor to change his shoes. There was something else on Will's mind.

"Larry," he said. "You ever been to a nursing home?"

"A nursing home?" He set the picture back on Will's bureau. "You mean where old people live?"

"Yeah. My mom's taking me to one tomorrow to see my grandfather. She says he has to stay in one for awhile, to get his strength back, before he comes home. I talk to him on the phone about once every other day, but only for a minute and I have to do most of the talking because it's hard for him to say anything. He runs out of breath real fast."

Larry nodded. "I went to a nursing home once," he said, "to visit my Great Aunt Flora. It was weird. All those old people. They were either staring at the walls or trying to grab you."

"Trying to grab you?"

"Yeah. My mother says they're starved for affection."

"Oh."

"I hugged an old lady once, to be nice, and she wouldn't let go. A nurse had to come and pry her off me."

Will was thinking that if anyone reached out to him, he'd just look straight ahead and pretend that he didn't see anything.

"It smells funny in there, too," Larry went on. "Like when they wash the bathrooms at school."

Will put on his old sneakers. "Did you ever go back?"

"No. I didn't have to. My Great Aunt Flora died."

"Gosh."

"It was kinda sad but she left my parents some money and that was good because my father was out of work for a long time."

"You never told me that!" Will exclaimed.

Larry looked at him and shrugged. "You never asked me."

Will tied his shoes, wondering if he should tell Larry about his father being out of work, too.

Larry peeled the rest of the dried fruit off its slick paper, made a ball out of it and popped the wad into his mouth. "What's with you, Will?"

Will stood up. "I haven't told anyone, Larry. Not at school anyway. Ms. Ritter knows because my mom told her. But my father has been out of work for over a year, He still doesn't have a job."

Larry stopped chewing. "But he's driving a moving van—"

"He was, but not anymore. And that guy never paid him."

Larry winced and resumed eating. He closed the baseball scrapbook and walked over to Will's shelves to put it away. Will wondered whether he had done the right thing, telling Larry.

Just then, Honkalot honked from behind the barn and both boys looked toward the window.

Larry brightened. "Hey, Will! Let's go make toast for Honkalot. Want to?"

Outside, the midafternoon air was quiet and cool. Overhead, the November sun hovered in a nest of haze. Larry carried the toast while Will hauled a large plastic bag across the yard. Now that Honkalot was better, he stayed in the barn.

"More Olney 3 square for you!" Will said, tossing the bag of grass on the floor beside the goose. "But I wish you'd start eating something else so Evelyn Potter wouldn't have to keep bringing this stuff in.

"She makes me feel obliged, you know? And she keeps asking if she can come over to see you." He screwed up his face. "I don't want any *girls* over here—except for Ms. Ritter!"

Larry giggled.

Honkalot opened his bill, anticipating the toast, but the boys teased him instead. Finally, Will handed over a piece and Honkalot's neck sprang forward, his bill snatching the bread in one swift motion. Larry was still a little timid around Honkalot and dropped his crust on the floor in front of the goose.

"Let's run up to the pond!" Will suggested.

The boys sprinted through the open back doors of the barn and took off into the pasture with Honkalot following. Now that the splint was off, the goose seemed to enjoy stretching out both wings as he ran. He tried hard to stay with the boys, but his webbed feet caught at lumps in the hard ground. Only when Will stopped to pick a milkweed pod did the goose catch up.

With his thumb, Will cracked open the fat, brown pod. It was crisp and broke easily. "Watch this!" he called to Larry who had raced on ahead. Larry stopped to see as Will blew into his hand and sent a swarm of white-tufted seeds flying into the air.

Like tiny, weightless feathers, the seeds drifted. The goose honked and Will whooped as they chased the fluffy, formless cloud through the pasture. Once, Will clapped his hands and waited for Honkalot to come to him, like a puppy, then picked him up and threw him into the air toward Larry. Honkalot flapped his wings, hard and fast, and coasted for a long moment covering several feet before smoothly descending to the ground.

The two boys looked at each other. "Wow," Will said quietly, unsure of how he really felt about this moment.

Honkalot tucked in his wings and returned to Will, who kneeled and waited, with an outstretched hand.

"You almost did it, Honkalot," he said, gathering the goose close to him. "You were almost flying!"

After Larry's mother picked him up, Will sat with Honkalot on a hay bale near the back door of the barn. It was already dark and the stars were out. Will chewed on a piece of straw and used it, from time to time, like a pointer. "That star there, Honkalot, is the North Star," he said. "And over there is the Big Dipper."

Honkalot honked and Will grinned.

"Did you know that Hercules lives in the sky, too? Grampa can find him." Will rearranged his legs and put an arm around his goose. "Grampa's really smart, you know. He taught me all about the stars. And about corn. *And* compost.

"He's my best friend, you know. Robbie's second. And Larry's third. Well…maybe Larry's second and Robbie's third."

Will threw down the piece of straw and plucked out another. For a moment, he was quiet.

"Grampa says if you fly, I should let you go," Will said finally. "He told me on the phone one day that a wild goose like you should be with its own kind. He said you'd never truly be happy living just with people."

Will sighed. "But I need you to stay."

He let the straw drop from his hand and looked back up at the sky. His hair was in his eyes but he left it there.

The goose honked.

"Grampa says the North Star is always moving, Honkalot. All the stars are moving."

Will pondered the sky.

"Grampa says that in a hundred thousand years, even the Big Dipper won't look the same."

Honkalot stretched his wings.

"I guess nothing ever stays the same, does it?"

16
A Room with a View

Larry was wrong about the smell. As Will and his mother walked the quiet, tiled hallway to Grampa's room, Will was reminded of macaroni, not bathrooms.

Not only that, but no one had yet reached out to him and there were plenty of old people in wheelchairs, lining the nursing home hallways like extra furniture.

"He drifts in and out, too," his mother was saying. She said she wanted to warn him. "One minute he's talking about the weather and telling me what he had for lunch, the next minute he's not making any sense at all. It's like he's confused. I want you to be prepared for that."

As they passed a man sitting in a wheelchair, Will summoned the courage to slow down and smile a little. He even started to say "hello." But the man rolled his head onto his shoulder and closed his eyes. Will clutched the pinecone turkeys he'd made for his grandfather and continued walking. It was a good thing they left the twins home with Mrs. Beardsley. They might have been scared.

"This way, Will," his mother said, guiding him around another corner.

"Does Grampa have his own room?" Will asked.

"No, he has a roommate," she said. "But he's next to the window so he has a room with a view."

When they walked in, the first thing they saw was an old man, asleep on his back, with his mouth open. Will's eyes darted to the next bed, where he was relieved to see Grampa sitting up watching television. Yet even from several feet away, Will could see the difference in his grandfather. He seemed smaller, his face pale and chalky, his eyes dark and sunken.

Will wanted to rush over and hug him, but he moved slowly, fearful that somehow Grampa had changed on the inside as well as on the outside.

"Hey," Grampa said. He lifted one hand and turned his head toward them. His voice was tremulous, but filled with recognition and warmth.

Will's mother turned off the TV and kissed Grampa on the cheek. Grampa smiled.

It was Will's turn. He set his turkeys on the windowsill and leaned over the clean white sheets to give his grandfather a delicate hug.

When he was settled in a chair beside the bed, he smiled up at his grandfather, but he was surprised to find himself searching for something to say.

"Did you see the turkeys I brought you, Grampa?"

His grandfather nodded. Will began to suspect that Grampa wouldn't be able to say much today.

But then his grandfather reached out to touch Will's hand. "How's…the goose?" he asked.

Will's face lit up with relief. Words came in a rush. "Just great, Grampa! I can't wait for you to see him. He's the greatest pet I've ever had. Actually, he's the only pet I've ever had! Isn't he, Mom?"

"I guess that's true," Will's mother added. "Poor Will. He was always asking for a dog, back in Baltimore." She stood back, with her coat on, near the window.

"A goose is wild, Will," Grampa said, and Will could tell the words were a struggle. When Grampa paused to take a deep breath, his chest rattled. "Remember…what I said?"

Will remembered all right. His grandfather wanted him to let it go. He pulled his hand away. This was not what he wanted to talk about.

"Did you know that Dad is in Vancouver now?" he asked. "He's going to work on another fishing boat, Grampa. He called Mom late last night."

Grampa looked over Will's head to Miriam. "You heard finally?…from Josh?" He sounded so surprised, so amazed that Will was confused.

He turned to his mother but she didn't answer Grampa's question. Just kind of stared at them both with such an empty, tired expression that a terrible feeling washed over Will.

Was it possible his mother had been lying to him? That she never got those late night phone calls? That, in fact, she hadn't heard from his father at all? That he was gone?

Will touched the edge of Grampa's bed as though to steady himself. All this time he had been bracing himself for the horror of this moment—and still it snuck up on him! Probably because he had been so busy—with school, with Honkalot, and lately, with Larry.

"You don't know where Dad is, do you, Mom?"

His mother met his gaze. Slowly, she shook her head.

"I think that when he lost yet another job he couldn't face us, Will. He let us down is what he kept saying to me on the phone. He's depressed. Deeply depressed."

"Maybe he just needs to prove to everybody that he can do another kind of job, but nobody gives him the chance!"

"Maybe. Maybe that's part of it," she said.

Will started to feel angry. "He never went to Seattle, did he, Mom?"

She shook her head. "No. But he did go to Fresno. California. I had a phone number there. He was staying with an old high school buddy. I begged him to come home again." She paused. "But I haven't heard. Not since. I suppose I could track him down if I had to, Will. But I can't keep begging him."

"Why didn't you tell me?" Will demanded.

"I don't know. To protect you, I guess. I didn't want you to be hurt anymore than you already have been."

"But why'd you have to lie?"

His mother turned away. It was Will's grandfather who answered. "Will…look at me."

Reluctantly, he did.

"You dad's lost," Grampa said, pausing to suck in his breath noisily. "Like your goose."

Gosh it hurt Will to see his grandfather struggle like this.

"Sometimes," Grampa went on. "When people lose a part of themselves...they have to go away...to find it again."

"He'll come back," Grampa said. "I know he will."

Will's mother came over and put a hand on Will's shoulder. "In my heart, I think he will, too," she said.

But Will wasn't so sure.

"You got no choice, son," Grampa said with great effort. "It's like your goose, Will...If you love him...you gotta let him go...so he can find his way."

Confused, Will stared at his hands, unsure of what to think or how to feel.

Grampa was straining, reaching with his hand for Will.

Out of the corner of his eye, Will watched. He put one hand on the bed and let Grampa pat it.

"That's my boy," Grampa said, taking a deep breath and laying back against his pillow.

But Will was still stuck on the words, "Let him go. Find his way." When Grampa said that, who did he mean? His father or his goose?

"Grampa has a lovely big window and a nice view," his mother said firmly, close to Will's ear. "Don't you think so, Will?"

Will nodded. His mother warned him about not upsetting Grampa. So he looked out the window, pretending to appreciate the view over a wide, flat lawn that was bordered by brown, frostbitten flower beds.

"Grampa says he sees rabbits come out everyday from under the hedge to nibble at the clover."

"Geese, too," Grampa added. "The river...the Susquehanna is... just below that rise." His words marched out slowly and seemed to reflect a faraway look in his eyes.

But Will knew the river wasn't there. He and his mother had

crossed it miles back, near Harrisburg. Besides, the geese wouldn't be coming over it now, not in late November. Then Will realized that this was Grampa's little joke, because of Honkalot.

He grinned and searched his grandfather's face for the twinkle in his eye. But Grampa's face remained impassive, his eyes vacant, staring. Sometimes, when he inhaled, it sounded like he was gasping for breath.

"Fly right over," Grampa said, waving his hand with a jerky motion at the ceiling.

Alarmed, Will looked at his mother but she was busy rearranging things on the table beside Grampa's bed. *He drifts in and out.* Is this what she meant?

"Thousands of 'em!" Grampa said.

Will reached over and took his grandfather's large hand in both of his own. The hand felt cool and lumpy. The skin on it seemed loose, almost translucent.

"F-fly right over," Grampa stammered.

"But it's a Bluebird Day," Will said softly, testing. "No clouds, Grampa. Just sunshine. Geese don't like to fly, remember?"

His grandfather didn't respond.

"It's time to go," Will's mother said. "Come on, Will, we still need to get you a haircut on the way home."

She leaned over the bed to kiss Grampa good-bye. "You take it easy," she told him. "We'll call you in the morning."

Grampa said nothing, just stared into the far corner of the room and drew another deep, noisy breath.

"You all set, Will? We don't want to tire him anymore."

Of course Will didn't want to tire his grandfather. But he didn't want to go yet either. Not with Grampa like this.

"Come on, Will," his mother urged.

Will squeezed his grandfather's hand once more and set it down softly on the bed, all the while hoping that Grampa would "drift back in" before they left. "Guess I have to say good-bye Grampa."

His mother had gathered her purse and was waiting in the doorway.

Will pushed his chair back against the wall. Then he turned to look at Grampa one last time and something occurred to him. Quickly, he reached into his pants pocket for the Optic Wonder, folded out the four lenses to make a pair of binoculars and returned to place it in his grandfather's hand.

"There," he said. His throat was tight and he had to whisper. "If those geese come down the river, Grampa, you can get a better look."

17
Letting Go

"I know it's only a picture," Sarah Lacey had apologized at school when she gave Will the painting. "But if you hang it over your goose's box maybe he'll feel less lonely."

It was early morning and the house was silent. Will lay in bed with his hands behind his head, staring at *Autumn Journey*. His mother wouldn't let him hang the picture in the barn near Honkalot. She said it was too nice. So Will hung it in his room on the only wall space he had, between the map and a poster of his favorite Oriole, Cal Ripken.

He hadn't talked to Grampa for three days now. The people at the nursing home said he was too tired. But the next time he and his mother visited, Will had decided, he would bring something from home, maybe the pipe rack, to warm up that room.

Will closed his eyes and time melted. He woke up smelling something good from downstairs. The twins were not in their cribs. It was almost nine o'clock. He wondered why his mother hadn't come in to wake him for school.

The hardwood floor was cold. Will put on his slippers. Downstairs, he was surprised to see Mrs. Beardsley in her apron, cooking sausage at the stove. Molly and Megan were on the floor, coloring.

"Mornin'!" Mrs. Beardsley chirped. "Don't you look handsome in that new haircut!" Will had forgotten about his haircut.

"Your Ma had to go into town this morning," Mrs. Beardsley said. She struggled to flip one of the sausage patties and a roll of fat jiggled under her arm. "She asked if I'd watch you and the girls until she got back. She'll run you up to school later."

"Where'd she go?" Will asked.

Grease was sputtering in the frying pan. Mrs. Beardsley had to step back. "Harrisburg. You ready to eat?"

"Harrisburg?" Will pulled out a chair. "What for?"

"To see a doctor, Will. I don't know who." She picked up a plate. "Now. How about you sit down and eat?"

A doctor? Will sat down. What was wrong with his mother?

"One patty or two, Will?" Mrs. Beardsley asked, her spatula poised over the frying pan.

"Two, please." The good smells had whetted his appetite. He had thirds of everything—eggs, sausage, toast. Afterward, upstairs, he helped change the twins' diapers and dressed them in matching red overalls. He decided Mrs. Beardsley wasn't so bad when you knew her a little better. At the very least, she was a good cook.

"They say we might have snow tomorrow," Mrs. Beardsley commented when everyone was back downstairs, dressed.

The thought of snow excited Will. Grampa had some great hills for sledding. Will could ask Larry to come over. If they cancelled school, maybe Larry could spend the night. "I hope it does snow!" Will exclaimed.

He sprawled on the living room floor and began to build a castle out of blocks for the twins while Mrs. Beardsley sat in one of the overstuffed chairs nearby knitting and watching them. She chuckled, it seemed, over everything they did.

"Wook at dis!" Molly said, putting a plastic pig on top of the castle.

"Wee see dis!" Megan said, pulling on Will's sleeve so he'd look at the cow sneaking in the castle's front door.

Both girls dissolved into giggles and together, knocked down the whole castle, just as Will's mother walked in. The girls jumped up and ran to her. Mrs. Beardsley put down her knitting and stood. Will looked at the fallen blocks and thought about rebuilding, but was sure he had to go to school now.

"Come on, girls," Mrs. Beardsley said. "I want to show you something I brought, but you have to come upstairs with me." Excited, the girls followed her.

Will finished tossing the blocks back in the basket while his mother came into the room and sat in a nearby chair. She seemed tired, quiet. Will was about to ask her what was wrong when he felt the presence of another person in the room. He turned toward the kitchen and was startled to see his father.

"I didn't mean to scare you," he said, taking a step into the room.

Will was so surprised he didn't even know how to react. "Dad," is all he said.

His father tried to smile. "I know you're probably angry at me. But I'm awfully glad to see you, son."

Will pushed himself up and stood. But it was his father who came to him first and hugged him hard. Will put his arms around his father, but the hold was tentative, uncertain, because Will didn't know whether to trust this moment. Something dark and uncertain still lingered. Something was being left unsaid. Will felt it just as surely as he felt the beating of his father's heart through his shirt.

Gently, he pushed himself away and turned to look at his mother who sat silently in the living room, her coat still on. He noticed she was holding the Optic Wonder in her hands.

And all at once, Will knew what it was that neither of his parents could tell him.

"Grampa?" he asked.

His mother's eyes, red-rimmed and sad, looked up at him. She nodded. "He went in his sleep, honey. In the night."

Will felt his father's hand on his back. "There was no pain," he said. "He wasn't even awake at the end."

Will went to his mother and took the Optic Wonder. He didn't even cry because at first he felt nothing, just a strange sort of numbness. But as the enormity of his loss gradually sank in, Will felt overwhelmed with a feeling of hopelessness. A warm wall of tears slowly built behind his eyes. His fists clenched and he dropped his head.

Will's mother stood and put her arms around him. "He left your dad the farm," she said, stroking the back of his head. "We're going to learn how to grow vegetables and soybeans, Will."

Will squeezed his eyes shut and let her press his face against her shoulder. His grandfather. What would they do without Grampa?

"When we knew Grampa probably wasn't going to make it, we took a good hard look at everything," his mother went on.

Will pulled back sharply, "What do you mean? You knew Grampa was going to die?"

She nodded weakly. "We knew a couple of days ago that it didn't look good. So I called Dad with that phone number I had in California, and I told him. He borrowed some money and flew home yesterday. He was with Grampa late last night, honey, when he passed away. That's when Dad called and I asked Mrs. Beardsley to come over. I didn't want to wake you up, Will. I thought about it. Dad and I even talked about it. But we decided it was better for you to remember Grampa that last day, when you talked to him. It's best…"

"Daddee! Daddee!" the twins called out, rushing down the stairs.

"Will, wait!" his mother said.

"Don't go!" his father called.

But Will was already out the door, running across the yard to the barn. He ran through the front doors and past the row of stanchions, startling Honkalot who called out for him from the sawdust bin. *Honk-a-ronk*!

Even then Will didn't stop. He kept running, as hard and as fast as he could, out the back door, through the barnyard, up into the pasture, pounding his feet against the old cow path in anger. He was angry that his parents hadn't told him Grampa would die. And even more angry that Grampa was gone.

He was halfway to the pond before realizing that Honkalot was beside him, flying—*flying*—silently, behind his right shoulder.

Still he ran, until he reached the top of the hill overlooking the pond. There, he sank to the ground, out of breath, and beat his fists against his thighs. "Noooooo!" he screamed, his plaintive cry the only sound in the thin, cool air.

Honkalot settled beside him and nudged him under the elbow. Reluctantly, Will put an arm around him. Then he gathered up the goose and cried into the feathers of his back.

A few years ago, when his grandmother passed away, Will was sick with flu and couldn't go to the funeral. But he was there the day Grampa buried his dog, Maggie, at the edge of the rose garden. He thought about it now, recalling the smell of the freshly turned earth, the yellow rose he had trouble picking and how Grampa, with one hand on the shovel handle, was talking to God. He wasn't really praying, or looking up to heaven or anything, just saying things out loud like, "Now you got you one fine Labrador retriever, Lord. You take good care of her, hear? Until I be up there, too."

Slowly, it became a comforting thought, knowing that Maggie was up there, waiting to whack her big black tail against Grampa. Maggie and Grandma, too. She'd be there with her apron on, waiting.

After a while Will stopped crying and realized how much he was shivering. In his rush to leave he hadn't taken a jacket. He released Honkalot and hugged himself, rubbing his arms to get warm. As he did, he gazed across the fields toward the river shining peacefully in the distance. Deep inside, Will knew that, like the Susquehanna, life would roll on. They would live at the farm. It was home now. He would go to school here.

And maybe, Will thought, just maybe, his father would be different. The farm would be his job—just as it had been Grampa's. They could sell corn in the summer and pumpkins in the fall. They could hay the fields and fill the barn with bales. Maybe Will could finally get the dog he always wanted. They could have a life here—a good life.

But it would never be the same without Grampa.

He started to cry again and Honkalot pecked him on the cheek, as though trying to dab away a tear. Will stroked the goose on its neck and looked up. Something about the sky seemed familiar and when he realized what it was, he started to smile. It was the same sky as the one in *Autumn Journey*, gray and cloudy, with lots of places for geese to hide. Definitely not a bluebird day. And then Will did smile because just thinking about a bluebird day and what it meant reminded him of Grampa at his best.

What he wouldn't give, Will thought, to plant one last kiss on Grampa's rough cheek, or squeeze that big lumpy hand once more. Or just sit beside him and breathe in some of that *wonderful* pipe smoke.

If only he'd known Grampa was going to die, he could have said good-bye—or done something to show him how much he loved him.

And suddenly, Will had an idea. It was not too late, he thought. Grampa's spirit was still winging its way to heaven. He was sure of it.

Will looked at Honkalot. There was only one thing left to do, he decided. He would do it, not only for the goose and his grandfather's spirit, but for himself, too. For restoration—or reparation—or whatever that word was from God that made Grampa plant the extra cornfield.

Will gathered up the goose one last time, savoring the feel of feathers against his damp cheek. "I'll always love you, Honkalot," he said. "But it's time for you to go back. To be with your family."

Slowly, Will stood with the bird in his arms and then quickly heaved it into the air. "Go!" he yelled. "Go on!"

Honkalot landed a few feet away and walked in a circle, bewildered, turning his head quickly, from side to side.

Will scooped up the goose again and tossed it into the air.

"Fly, Honkalot! You can make it to Maryland today if you fly fast enough! Follow the river! It's not far! Go on! Before it snows!"

This time, the goose flapped its wings and flew. "Go on!" Will hollered as he ran at the goose, arms flailing. When the goose tried to land again, Will kicked loose a chunk of sod and threw it. "Get out of here!"

The goose circled overhead. Will wiped at the fresh tears gathering on his cheek and picked up a stone. "Keep going!" he ordered.

"Please don't stop," he begged.

The goose flew on. Will dropped the stone and pulled out the Optic Wonder to get a closer look. Right now, Honkalot was higher than Will had ever seen him before. "Be careful," he murmured.

While he was watching, the wind picked up and Will heard

a voice—his name—from far away. For a second, he might have believed it was Grampa, calling out "that's my boy" from heaven, if he hadn't turned in the very next breath to see one of his parents waving to him. Whoever it was was a tiny dark speck against the barn's dull red boards.

Honkalot was making a wide circle. "Don't come back," Will said under his breath, even though a part of him desperately wished for it. The goose continued its circle, however, and flew on, toward the river.

Will swallowed hard. There would be no more guilt for taking this goose from the sky. Its flight was continuing where it had left off two months before. The reparation was complete.

And yet, as he watched it fly away, Will felt a twinge inside. He figured there would always be a twinge deep inside, where the sore spot used to be. With a gentle, back-and-forth motion of his wrist, he waved one final time.

When he turned the Optic Wonder back toward the barn, he could see that it was his father coming up through the pasture. He was running. Will focused and watched as his father crested the next hill and stopped to hold up something very small. It was slender and kind of white and silver, like an ink pen.

Or a spark plug, Will suddenly realized.

As he stood in the cold November air with tears burning his cheeks, a smile slowly spread across his face. Will lowered the Optic Wonder. Then he took of running, headlong, down the slope to meet his father.

Gray Feather honks. The wind, whistling in his ears, carries the sweet harmony of earth and sky.

The mighty Susquehanna rolls to the south, beckoning, and Gray Feather follows. His wings, heavy at first, now stroke with grace and ease, as though finally recalling the familiar rhythm of a once forgotten song.

He dips his head to glance at the hilltop where the boy waves like a single, tiny flower in the breeze. At the same time, a cool tail wind pushes him toward the river. Gray Feather has to fight it to circle around. Far below, treetops sway in the breeze and wild currents of dark water ripple the surface of the river, driving against each other, like rivers within the river.

Something ancient and mysterious tugs at Gray Feather, whispering with the wind that the invisible pathway will take him downstream to where the river and the bay become one with water and geese. A warm pocket of air surrounds him, pulling him, and Gray Feather lets himself be taken.

Up ahead the sky is gray and leaden. Thick, low clouds gathered by the wind drift to a stop, blotting out the sun and settling across the horizon like large sleeping animals. Below the dip and pull of his wings, nothing but the river moves.

Gray Feather flies on sensing only what the boy knows so well. It is a good day for flying.